"Let me l familiar."

"I will."

Blondie was unusually silent as Tucker continued farther into the woods. They had gone another twenty yards when the beam of his flashlight picked up a dark mound on the ground.

"I need you to stay here by this tree, understand?"

"What? Why?" When she sucked in a harsh breath, he knew she'd spied the mound, too.

Without saying anything more, he carefully approached the oddly shaped heap. As he grew closer, he knew there was no mistake.

A dead body.

And oddly, there wasn't nearly as much blood on the ground as he would have expected to find if the guy had been killed in this spot.

Yet the dead guy had to be the source of the blood on Blondie's clothes. Before he could turn to ask her about it, she came up behind him.

"Who is he?" she asked in a whisper.

"Funny, I was going to ask you the same thing." He turned to pin her with a fierce gaze. "Did you kill him?"

Her eyes widened. But she didn't deny committing the crime.

A crack of gunfire rang out. He hit the ground, rolled and aimed his weapon to return fire.

As Blondie took off running.

Laura Scott has always loved romance and read faith-based books by Grace Livingston Hill in her teenage years. She's thrilled to have been given the opportunity to retire from thirty-eight years of nursing to become a full-time author. Laura has published over thirty books for Love Inspired Suspense. She has two adult children and lives in Milwaukee, Wisconsin, with her husband of thirty-five years. Please visit Laura at laurascottbooks.com, as she loves to hear from her readers.

Books by Laura Scott

Love Inspired Suspense

Hiding in Plain Sight
Amish Holiday Vendetta
Deadly Amish Abduction
Tracked Through the Woods
Kidnapping Cold Case
Guarding His Secret Son

Texas Justice

Texas Kidnapping Target
Texas Ranger Defender

Mountain Country K-9 Unit

Baby Protection Mission

Dakota K-9 Unit

Chasing a Kidnapper

Visit the Author Profile page at LoveInspired.com for more titles.

TEXAS RANGER DEFENDER

LAURA SCOTT

If you purchased this book without a cover you should be aware that this book is stolen property. It was reported as "unsold and destroyed" to the publisher, and neither the author nor the publisher has received any payment for this "stripped book."

ISBN-13: 978-1-335-95728-3

Texas Ranger Defender

Copyright © 2025 by Laura Iding

All rights reserved. No part of this book may be used or reproduced in any manner whatsoever without written permission.

Without limiting the author's and publisher's exclusive rights, any unauthorized use of this publication to train generative artificial intelligence (AI) technologies is expressly prohibited.

This is a work of fiction. Names, characters, places and incidents are either the product of the author's imagination or are used fictitiously. Any resemblance to actual persons, living or dead, businesses, companies, events or locales is entirely coincidental.

For questions and comments about the quality of this book, please contact us at CustomerService@Harlequin.com.

® is a trademark of Harlequin Enterprises ULC.

Love Inspired
22 Adelaide St. West, 41st Floor
Toronto, Ontario M5H 4E3, Canada
www.LoveInspired.com

Printed in Lithuania

The Lord is my light and my salvation;
whom shall I fear? the Lord is the strength of my life;
of whom shall I be afraid?
—*Psalm* 27:1

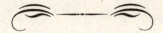

This book is dedicated to all those in
law enforcement who put their lives on the line
every day. You have my utmost admiration and respect.

ONE

Run. Don't stop. Run!

The light glowing in the darkness from the window looming in the distance seemed too far away. She feared she'd never get there in time. She'd been running for what seemed like forever.

Fear gripped her chest like a vise, making it difficult to breathe. Her head throbbed painfully with each step, but she ignored the discomfort. Her head hurt. Her entire body hurt. But that didn't matter.

Keep moving. Don't stop or he'll find you.

Pushing herself as hard as she could, she burst out of the trees into the open. The pungent scent of cows and horses indicated she was on a ranch of some sort.

There was no way to know if the soft light from the window would provide a badly needed sanctuary or not. As she was in the middle of nowhere, she didn't have much of a choice but to find out.

Please Lord, guide me! Show me the way!

The crack of gunfire nearly stopped her heart. Throwing herself to the ground, she frantically searched for something, anything to use for cover.

There was nothing but grass, a wooden plank fence and the ranch house.

After several long moments of silence, she sprang to her feet and set off running again in a zigzag pattern that she hoped would make her a more difficult target. With a renewed sense of urgency—gunfire was a powerful motivator—she ducked behind the wooden fence, then managed to reach the side of the house.

Rather than going to the front door, she hurried to the lighted window. Peering inside, she saw a tall man tucking blankets around a frail figure lying in a bed.

The wave of relief was staggering. Anyone willing to care for someone else couldn't be all bad. She pounded on the window frame, causing the tall man to look sharply at her. Then he quickly crossed the room and pushed the window upward, peering at her through the screen.

"Who are you?" The guy's sandy-brown hair was cut short, and he wore the typical Western shirt favored by many Texans, along with jeans and cowboy boots. He didn't look the least bit happy to see her. "What are you doing out there?"

"I'm in danger." She ignored the first part of his question, because her mind didn't seem to be working properly. Who was she? Good question, because her name didn't come to the tip of her tongue. "Did you hear the gunshot? I—that was meant for me."

"I heard it." He scowled, looking behind her. Then he lifted the screen and held out his hand. "Climb in, then."

"Thank you." She took his hand, tears springing to her eyes at the gentle strength of his fingers. It seemed like an eternity since she'd been able to trust someone not to hurt her. Moving awkwardly, she threw one leg over the windowsill, then ducked through.

"Why in tarnation is someone climbing in the window?"

an elderly voice rasped. "Don't people use the front door anymore?"

"Everything is fine, Pops. We'll be out of your hair shortly." The calming words were as much of a balm to her ragged nerves as the stranger's warm hand had been.

She stood in the room, shivering. Autumn in south Texas was still warm, so she must be in shock. The tall stranger peered out the window for a long moment, then closed and locked it.

Glancing at the frail man, she forced a smile. "I'm so sorry to intrude."

"You'all aren't intruding." While the older man's body appeared weak, his gaze was sharp, and a smile tugged at his mouth. "Most excitement I've had in weeks."

"Get some rest, Pops. Come with me, Ms.—" The sandy-haired man arched a brow as he gestured to the bedroom door.

"I—uh…" She tried to come up with a name, but again her mind was a complete blank. Rather than answering, she quickly left the room, then paused in the hallway outside the bedroom door. "Which way?"

"To the right." The man's gaze drilled into hers. "What's your game?"

"Game?" She turned, following the hallway to what appeared to be a large open concept kitchen. The place was very nice, but the distrust radiating from the tall stranger indicated she was on shaky ground.

"What happened? Are you'all in some sort of trouble?" He gestured to a stool at the counter. Then he abruptly frowned. "Wait a minute. Is that blood?"

"Blood?" Dazed, she glanced down at herself, noticing for the first time that there were dark crimson smears staining her light gray T-shirt. And there were smaller smears of blood on her hands and bare arms. She lifted a shaky hand to the back of her head, the source of her throbbing pain, feeling the large goose egg there. But there was no break in the skin to account for the blood. She sank into the closest chair, her mind whirling. "I don't think it's mine."

"Yeah, I'm getting that," the man drawled. "My name is Tucker Powell, and I'm a Texas Ranger. I need to know your name and what happened out there."

Despite his annoyed glare and equally imposing stature, she was relieved to know Tucker Powell was a Texas Ranger. Yet her moment of gratitude was short-lived.

"I don't know." She fingered the lump on the back of her head. "I'm sorry, but I don't know who I am or what happened. All I can tell you is that I'm in danger."

Tucker's eyes narrowed to slits. He took a quick step toward her, and she reacted instinctively by shrinking away from him, lifting her arm to ward off a blow.

He abruptly stopped. He raised his hands, palms forward. "Whoa. I'm not going to hurt you."

Wasn't he? How would she know? Wave after wave of despair washed over her.

She didn't know anything. Whose blood stained her clothes. Or who'd fired a gun at her. Not even something as simple as her name!

And the latter was the most frightening thing of all.

Tuck forced himself to stay back, giving the scared and skittish woman enough room that she might feel safe. As a Texas Ranger, he'd dealt with a wide variety of crimes. But this was the first time a crime had shown up on his doorstep.

Or in this case, a window. Either way, he wasn't buying into this woman's story.

"I'm not going to hurt you," he repeated. "But I need to know who you are and who is after you." He also needed to know whose blood was staining her clothing, but decided not to point that out again. "I can't keep you safe if I don't understand the threat against you."

"I don't know." She lowered her chin to her chest, her long, tangled blond hair hiding her features. After a full minute, she lifted her gaze to his. He was struck by the brightness of her blue eyes. "I understand how this sounds. I only know I'm in danger."

He didn't doubt her claim of being in danger. The gunshot was proof of that. No, it was the *why* that mattered. Was she a victim of a crime? Or the perpetrator? He'd seen a lot in his law enforcement career, and a beautiful face did not always equate innocence.

He noticed how she lifted a hand to the back of her head. "What's wrong?"

"I have a large lump on the back of my head." She frowned. "Could I bother you for an ice pack?"

He crossed to his grandfather's freezer and pulled out a bag of frozen peas. "Do you mind if I take a look?"

"Go ahead." She sounded resigned and exhausted. Her clothing was stained with blood and dirt, making him wonder how far she'd traveled to reach his grandfather's ranch house.

Doing his best not to appear threatening, he moved closer and gently parted the hair on the back of her skull. The large lump was unmistakable, verifying her claim. He gently pressed the bag of frozen peas to the injury, causing her to let her breath out in a low hiss.

"Hurts?"

"Yes." She reached up to hold the peas in place. "But I'll be fine."

Would she? He wasn't as confident. Stepping back, he eyed her critically. "If you really can't remember anything, we'll need to head to the hospital." He gestured to the lump on her head. "You might have bleeding into your brain."

"No hospital." The words were sharp and clipped. "I just need time to regroup. To rest. I'm sure my memory will return in the morning."

Again, he wasn't convinced. But the hour was well past ten o'clock at night, and the closest hospital was a solid seventy-minute ride to San Antonio. Maybe a good night's sleep was all this mystery woman needed.

"Please," she whispered, suddenly looking exhausted and weak. "I need time to rest."

Maybe he was the one with a weakness, because he already knew he wasn't going to kick her out. At least, not yet.

"Do you have a weapon? Or anything sharp?" Her bare arms didn't show signs of drug use, but the bloodstains put his cop instincts on full alert.

"What? No!" She looked horrified for a moment, then slid off the stool to stand before him. After setting the frozen peas aside, she lifted her slender arms from her sides. "You can search me."

"I will." She looked surprised yet resigned as he did a quick pat down. The pockets of her jeans were empty, no knife and no belt or ankle holster holding a gun. No ID or cash, either. "Okay. I have some clothes you can change into."

"Oh, you're married." Relief flooded her eyes.

He quirked a brow. "I'm not. They belong to my sister. Are you married? Or engaged?"

"I don't think so." She looked at her left hand, as if to reassure herself she wasn't wearing a wedding or engagement ring. Then she touched a gold chain around her neck, tugging on it until a plain gold cross appeared. "I have this, but nothing else. I was afraid I'd have to trade it for a ride."

"A ride where?" He tried to sound casual, but her comment indicated she'd had a destination in mind.

"I—uh, I'm not sure." She frowned again. "I—I don't know how to explain it. I feel as if the memory is there, hovering in a gray mist just out of reach."

She was either an exceptional actress or she was telling the truth. Since he had absolutely no experience with people suffering from memory loss, he couldn't decide which.

"Do you want something to eat? Or drink?" His mother had passed away a few years ago, but she would have been horrified if he didn't offer a guest in need something to eat.

"Yes, please. Water and maybe toast?" She looked hesitantly around the kitchen, putting a hand to her belly. "I feel a little sick, but I'm not sure if that's because I'm hungry or the head injury."

"Possibly both." He moved toward the cupboard. "How about some chicken noodle soup to go with that toast?"

"That would be great. Thank you." To his shock, her eyes welled with tears. She abruptly brushed them away and reached for the bag of peas, then pressed it against her head. "Sorry. Delayed reaction."

Delayed reaction to what, exactly? He didn't voice the question, but set about heating up the soup and making toast. Tuck considered calling his fellow Texas Ranger buddies—Sam Hayward, Jackson Woodlow or Marshall Branson—for assistance, then decided to wait until morning.

He set the steaming bowl of soup and plate of buttered toast in front of her at the breakfast bar. She smiled, then bowed her head, clasping her hands together. "Dear Lord, thank You for this food and for keeping me safe in Your care. Amen."

Her prayer caught him off guard. Not that he hadn't ever seen anyone praying before a meal before, because he had. It was the way she'd prayed without thinking about it. As if she did so on a regular basis. Which was interesting, since she couldn't provide her first and last names.

While his mystery woman ate, he moved from one window to the next, peering outside to make sure there was nothing amiss. While he'd heard the retort of gunfire, it had been muffled enough to make him believe the person firing the weapon wasn't close.

Yet, if there was a shooter following Blondie, he needed to make sure he or she wasn't still out there. The minute he had her situated in his sister's room, he'd head out to check the perimeter.

"This was delicious, thanks."

He turned from the window to notice she had finished her soup and her toast. "I'm glad. Here, let me show you to your room."

She stood, then followed him down the hall past his grandfather's room to the next door on the left. "This is the bathroom. And this is Stacy's room." He and his sister had been taking turns looking after Pops over the past few months since his grandfather's health had taken a turn for the worse. He entered her room, opened the dresser drawers then turned to face her. "Help yourself. I need your bloodstained clothes though, when you're finished changing."

"Need them?" She frowned. "Why?"

"Because the blood is evidence." He gestured to her stained clothing. "You appear to have been involved in a crime. One that we'll need to report to the local authorities."

"Report what? That I can't remember what happened?" Her voice rose with agitation. Was it guilt that made her loathe to contact the authorities?

Then again, she hadn't been upset to learn he was a Ranger.

"That's why we're not doing anything tonight. I'm sure you'll feel better by morning." At least, he hoped her memory loss would be short-lived. He wasn't sure what would happen if she didn't remember her own name the following day. "As a Texas Ranger, I must insist you provide me those bloody garments."

She sighed. "Okay."

He nodded and turned to leave, giving her the privacy she deserved. He took a moment to crack the door and tiptoe inside his grandfather's room to make sure he was sleeping. Smiling at the low rumble of Pops's snoring, Tuck stepped back into the hall and closed the door.

He detoured to his room to grab his sidearm and a heavy-duty flashlight. Then he went through the kitchen to the mudroom. After settling his cowboy hat on his head, he slipped outside.

The Rocking T Ranch had been handed down from Tuck's grandmother's side of the family. Her maiden name had been Tucker, which is how he'd gotten his first name. The Rocking T was located roughly fifteen miles north of Cotton Springs, with the next largest city being San Antonio. With a condition as serious as a concussion and amnesia, he was inclined to take the injured woman to the larger city for care.

Outside, he continued scanning the area as he made his way around to the south side of the property, the general direction he assumed Blondie had taken to arrive at his grandfather's bedroom window. Hearing a noise from behind him, he whirled around, bringing his weapon and flashlight up into a ready position.

"Where are you going?" the woman asked fearfully,

squinting against the light shining in her eyes. She had changed her clothes, and he found it telling that she'd chosen a black short-sleeved shirt and black jeans from his sister's closet. As if she knew she needed to blend into the darkness.

"Go back inside," he ordered gruffly, lowering the gun. "I'm just checking to make sure no one is lurking nearby."

"I'm coming with you." She hurried forward. "Please. I need to know what's going on, too."

Since he couldn't very well force her into going back to the house, he gave a curt nod. "Fine. But stay behind me."

"Okay." Her voice was barely a whisper, and she grabbed the back of his shirt, as if she feared they'd get separated.

Wishing again that he had Marsh, Jackson or Sam there as backup, he moved silently past the fenced corral to the rugged area beyond.

"I came this way," the blonde woman whispered. "I saw the light from your grandfather's window."

"Do you remember anything else?" He glanced over his shoulder.

"I was scared. I knew I had to keep running so he wouldn't catch me."

"So who wouldn't catch you?" he asked.

"I don't know." She tightened her grip on his shirt. "You asked what I remembered."

"Yeah, well, I was hoping for something more specific." He hadn't meant to sound so sarcastic. "Do you remember how far you came?"

"Not exactly, although this area looks familiar."

He gave up, sensing he wasn't going to get details from Blondie until her memory returned.

If her memory returned. Or if she even bothered to tell him once her memory returned.

Shaking off his negative thoughts, he continued moving across the ranch property toward the grove of trees that were roughly fifty yards from the corral. Sweeping his flashlight over the ground, he didn't find a blood trail. But he easily took note of the broken branches, crushed leaves and flattened ground left by Blondie.

"Does this look familiar?" he asked in a low voice.

"Yes. I know I came through these trees." She tugged on his shirt to stop him. He turned to look at her, and she gestured to the ranch behind them. "You can't see it now, but the light from your grandfather's window was a beacon."

He could imagine her shaking with fear and running straight toward the light. Glancing at her, he nodded. "Okay, let me know if anything else looks familiar."

"I will."

Turning away from the ranch house, he continued following the not-so-subtle trail.

Blondie was unusually silent as he pushed farther into the woods. They had gone about another twenty yards when the beam of his flashlight picked up a dark mound on the ground. Something solid. He stopped so quickly, Blondie bumped into his back.

"What is it?" she asked in a whisper.

The tiny hairs on the back of his neck lifted in alarm. The mound up ahead almost looked like a body, but he couldn't be sure in the darkness. He reached behind his back and grabbed her arm. "I need you to stay here by this tree, understand?"

"What? Why?" When she sucked in a harsh breath, he knew she'd spied the mound, too.

Without saying anything more, he carefully approached the oddly shaped heap. As he grew closer, he knew there was no mistake.

A dead body. He played his light over the figure, noting the dark hair, dark clothing and the knife that protruded from the man's stomach. He reached forward to check a pulse, despite the guy's pale, waxy skin and lack of breathing.

There was nothing. In fact, the body was cold to the touch, as if it had been there for a while. Maybe even several hours.

And oddly, there wasn't nearly as much blood on the ground as he would have expected to find if the guy had been killed in this spot.

Yet the dead guy had to be the source of the blood on Blondie's clothes. Before he could turn to ask her about it, she came up behind him.

"Who is he?" she asked in a whisper.

"Funny, I was going to ask you the same thing." He turned to pin her with a fierce gaze. "Did you kill him?"

Her eyes widened as she stared past him at the man lying on the ground. But she didn't deny committing the crime.

A crack of gunfire rang out. He hit the ground, rolled and aimed his weapon to return fire.

As Blondie took off running.

TWO

Between the gunfire and the dead body, she caved to the desperate need to get away. To run. To hide.

Had she killed a man? The fog in her mind hadn't dissipated one bit. She honestly didn't know!

Tucker's accusation whirled in her mind as she ran, desperate to get far away from the dead man and sound of gunfire. Even though she'd washed up in the bathroom, she imagined the poor man's blood was still on her.

Who else's blood could it be?

Hearing the pounding footsteps behind her, she burst forward as fast as she could. At some level, she noticed the rest of the night was silent. Had the gunman killed Tucker?

The way she'd killed the unknown man?

How? Why? Her mind refused to bring up the image of what must have been a scuffle between them.

A hand grabbed her from behind, and suddenly she was falling to the ground, a heavy weight pinning her down. She tried to squirm away, but it was impossible.

"Stay down," Tucker said in a harsh whisper. "Don't make yourself a target."

Some of her fear and desperation eased. Maybe because it seemed as if Tucker had come after her to protect her.

Despite the way he'd accused her of murder.

The seconds ticked by slowly as silence engulfed them. After what seemed like an eternity, Tucker eased himself up on his elbows. "We're heading back to the ranch, okay? The barn is closer so that will be our first stop."

Her throat was tight with fear, making it impossible to respond.

"Blondie? Did you hear me?"

Blondie? She wanted to snap at him for the nickname. Then again, what else was he going to call her?

"Yes." She pushed the word through her constricted throat. "We're going back to the ranch, but we'll get to the barn first."

He hesitated, then rose to a crouch. Her arms trembled as she pushed herself upright. As much as the gunfire had scared her, she couldn't get the dead man out of her mind.

She wanted to believe she wouldn't have stabbed the man if she hadn't been fighting for her life. The bump on the back of her head might explain a physical altercation. At least, that's what she tried to tell herself.

But seeing the dead body had chilled her to the bone. As if not remembering her own name wasn't bad enough, she had to face the fact she may have taken another person's life.

Dear Lord Jesus, guide me! Heal my mind while keeping me safe in Your care!

"Ready?" There was a hint of impatience in Tucker's tone.

"Yes." She forced herself to move toward the dark shadow of the barn located to the left of the ranch house. Tucker stayed behind her, even grabbing her when she stumbled over a rock.

By the time they reached the side of the barn, a sense of relief washed over her, knowing they were safe.

The feeling was short-lived.

"What happened back there?" Tucker asked harshly. "Did you draw me to the dead body to set up an ambush?"

"What?" She gaped in shock. "No! I followed you outside, remember?"

"I remember. You're the one who can't recall important details, like your name or if you killed that guy."

"I didn't. At least, I don't think so." Her voice sounded weak to her own ears. "I wish I could remember, but I can't. I wish…" What was the point? Wishes meant nothing.

A man was dead. And she had no idea if she had been the one to stab him.

"Okay, stay close. I'm hoping the gunman took off, but there's no way to know for sure." Tucker pulled his cell phone from his pocket. After a moment, he said, "Marsh? Any chance you can round up Jackson and Sam and get to the Rocking T as soon as possible? I have…a bit of a situation and could use your help."

She didn't hear the other end of the conversation, but assumed the man named Marsh had answered in the affirmative as Tucker ended the call.

"It's going to take some time for my Ranger buddies to get here." He held her gaze for a long moment. "I'll need to get the Diamond County Sheriff's Department involved, too."

She swallowed hard, understanding the implication. "They're going to arrest me, aren't they?"

"I don't know." He got points for answering honestly. "They'll gather your bloody clothes as evidence and see if the blood matches that of the dead man."

"Then they'll arrest me," she repeated dully. Her head was throbbing again, and she would give just about anything to lie down and rest.

Preferably in a regular bed, not a hard cot within a jail cell.

"I really need you to tell me what happened out here. I can help if this was a case of self-defense."

If? Did he really think she went around stabbing people for the fun of it? Then again, what was he supposed to think when she couldn't remember her own name?

"I don't know." She was tired of repeating herself. "You can ask me ten more times and my answer will be the same."

He sighed, glancing back in the direction of where they'd found the dead man. "Okay, I need you to get inside the house. I don't know if that gunshot was meant for us or if someone else was the intended victim. I'm staying out here to keep an eye on things."

Telling herself there was no reason to be afraid, she nodded and turned away. Then she paused to glance back at him. "It's possible that the dead man attacked me, and I stabbed him in self-defense. But that doesn't explain the shooter. It seems logical whoever fired at me earlier is the same one who shot at us near the body."

He frowned as he digested that. "You could be right."

She hoped and prayed she was. Because having two different gunmen out there shooting at her was almost as disturbing as seeing the dead man.

As she moved along the side of the barn toward the ranch house, she heard Tucker making the phone call to the sheriff's department.

Sealing her fate.

A hint of movement near the edge of the ranch house caught her eye. A chill raced down her spine, and she stopped midstride.

Was someone there? Her brief glimpse at Tucker's grandfather made it clear he didn't have the strength and agility for a midnight stroll.

She stared at the location where she thought she'd seen movement, but whatever she'd seen was gone.

Or hiding.

Had the gunman made a loop around the property to ambush them here?

The overwhelming sense of apprehension was crippling.

She turned to head back toward Tucker, when she noticed another shift in the darkness. She ducked just as the crack of gunfire rang out. Louder this time, indicating the shooter was close.

Once again, she was flat on the ground, her arms covering her head as she waited for the impact of a bullet.

"Blondie!" Tucker's voice held concern.

She tried to answer, but her throat was so tight only a weird croaking sound emerged.

"Blondie! Are you hit?" Tucker's tone was frantic. "Where are you?"

"Here." She lifted her head an inch. At least wearing black had helped provide cover. "I'm okay. But he's around the corner of the ranch house!"

"Stay down!" Tucker's tone held a note of authority. Then she heard the thud of his footsteps as he went back to the ranch house at a dead run, no doubt fearing for his grandfather's well-being.

Her fault. She remained stretched out on the ground, sick with the realization she'd brought danger to their doorstep. If anything happened to his frail grandfather, she'd never forgive herself.

All she could do was to pray.

Please, Lord Jesus, keep Tucker and his grandfather safe in Your care!

Praying brought a slight measure of peace, although her heart still hammered against her ribs. Listening intently, she tried to imagine what was happening back at the ranch house.

The silence went on for what seemed like forever. After hearing muffled thumps and snapping twigs, she lifted her head up to see better.

But the area between her and the ranch house appeared empty.

More rustling sounds made her tense. Had the gunman doubled back to find her?

She didn't move, not even to take a breath. Only when the sounds stopped did she let out a silent sigh.

Stay or run? Tucker had told her to stay put, but she was feeling more vulnerable by the second. The grass around her wasn't that long, and she feared the gunman would be on top of her at any moment.

"Blondie? Are you okay?"

Tucker's voice was the strength she needed. Gathering her courage, she lifted her head. "Yes."

"I don't see anyone here now," Tucker went on. "You can get up. I'll cover you."

She gladly pushed herself up to her hands and feet. Then she ran toward Tucker and the safety of the ranch house.

Thankfully, she didn't hear gunfire or see anyone as she closed the gap. Upon reaching Tucker, she had to resist the urge to throw herself into his arms.

"Let's get you inside." He took her hand.

She nodded in agreement.

Once they were back in the kitchen, he eyed her critically. "I need you to stay inside to help keep an eye on my grandfather while I try to track the shooter."

"I understand." She glanced around nervously, searching

for a weapon. When her gaze landed on the block of knives, she turned away, remembering with too much clarity the knife that had protruded from the dead man's abdomen. "I—uh, don't have a phone to call 911, though."

"Good point. Hang on." He disappeared down the hall and into his grandfather's bedroom, then emerged less than a minute later with a small, older-model smartphone. "Here. This will work in a pinch." He handed her the device and gave her the code to access the home screen. "My number is under my name."

"This will work." She tried to smile. "Be careful out there, okay? I'm worried that guy will come back."

"Yeah. One more thing." He left the kitchen again, then returned with a long double-barreled shotgun. "It's loaded. I expect you to only use this in an emergency."

She took the weapon, keeping the barrels pointed at the floor. After cracking the barrel to verify there were two shells loaded, she closed it again. Oddly, the weapon didn't feel foreign in her hands. She must have held a gun like this before. "I understand. I will only use it if someone tries to hurt me or your grandfather."

"Exactly." He held her gaze for a long moment, then turned away. "Oh, and Blondie?"

"Yes?"

He offered a crooked smile. "Try not to shoot me."

Her eyes widened in horror before she realized he was teasing. She was not in the mood for jokes. She gave a curt nod as she dropped onto the closest breakfast bar stool.

Tucker left through the mudroom. After a moment, she rose and followed to make sure the door was locked behind him.

Then she returned to the main living space. Forgoing the kitchen, she sank into the overstuffed sofa. She set the shotgun across her lap, then rested her head back against the cushion.

Closing her eyes, she tried for what seemed like the hundredth time to remember who she was. What had happened to her and how she'd gotten here.

But the swirling mist in her mind persisted, revealing nothing that would keep her from being tossed in jail.

Tucker stood outside his grandfather's ranch house, listening intently. The shooter had tried to kill Blondie three times in a matter of hours. And the perp had gotten too close to the house for comfort.

Moving slowly and cautiously, he examined the area for clues. There was a partial footprint in the mud near the fence line, and he quickly took a picture with his phone. Then he checked the barn, even though he felt certain the horses would have let him know if there was anyone hiding inside.

He stayed in the shadows as he eased toward the area where they'd found the dead body. Oddly, he found it difficult to believe his mystery woman had stabbed him. Or if she had, he felt certain it had been an act of self-defense. The way she had shied away, as if expecting to be struck, made him angry. Clearly, she'd been hit before. Even if she couldn't remember it.

Yet the logical part of his mind warned him not to make any snap judgments. For one thing, the Mexican drug cartels had recently begun training women and children as assassins and drug traffickers. Even children as young as seven years old were trained to shoot a gun and become soldiers. While heartbreaking, it was also a clear warning not to take anything at face value.

And that included a woman who prayed before meals and wore a Christian cross around her neck.

Tuck forced himself to move slowly and silently toward the wooded area, making sure the gunman wasn't hiding nearby. He'd already been caught off guard once, and he wasn't anxious to be fired upon again.

In truth, he was convinced Blondie was the intended target. The third attempt to shoot her made him think she was a witness to something the gunman didn't want her to report to the police.

The shooter had no way of knowing she'd lost her memory.

Hopefully, the guy had taken off. When his phone vibrated in his pocket, he removed the device, relieved to see Marsh's name on the screen.

"I'm five minutes out. Sam and Jackson are busy but can free themselves up tomorrow if needed. Everything okay?" Marsh asked.

"Not even close. There's a gunman lurking nearby. I've circled the property without seeing him, but you know how that goes." He hadn't given Marsh the entire story of Blondie showing up with bloodstained clothes and no memory of what had transpired. Or the dead guy, for that matter. "The situation is fluid. I'll meet you'all out front to explain."

"I can hardly wait," Marsh drawled. "I'll be there soon." He ended the call.

As much as Tucker wanted to head back out to stand guard over the dead man, he decided to turn back to the ranch house to meet up with Marsh. Despite being convinced the shooter was long gone, Tuck wouldn't be able to relax until he had backup.

Using the five minutes to walk the perimeter for the

third time, he was glad to find nothing unusual. Glancing at his watch, he made his way back around to the front of the ranch house.

He resisted the urge to peek through the window to see what Blondie was up to. It wasn't lost on him that he'd provided a possible murder suspect with a weapon.

One she could easily use against him.

Yet what else could he have done? Leave her and Pops alone and vulnerable in the house? The gunman had targeted her three separate times. He'd trusted his gut, while hoping he wasn't being played for a fool.

The sooner Marsh and the others got here, the better. Scanning the horizon, he nearly sighed in relief when he saw the hint of light in the distance. The vehicle grew close enough for him to make out the twin headlights slowly growing brighter and brighter as the SUV bounced along the long driveway.

Marsh had made good time. Knowing his friend, he suspected he'd put pedal to the metal with blatant disregard of the posted speed limit.

When Marsh braked to a stop, Tuck hurried over. "Thanks for getting here so fast."

"Anytime." Marsh slid out from behind the wheel. "Care to fill me in?"

"Yeah." He glanced around the ranch house, then led the way around back. "A woman showed up here about an hour ago, her clothes stained with blood. She claims she doesn't remember anything, not even her own name." He eyed Marsh, who looked skeptical. "I know, it's quite the story. But that's not the end of it. Prior to her arrival, I heard a gunshot. It seemed to be far away. I thought it could have been from the Wandering Willow Ranch to the northwest. Everyone shoots at coyotes out here."

"And now you think the gunshot was meant for the woman with amnesia?"

"Exactly." Tuck continued scanning their surroundings as he spoke. If the shooter was nearby, Tuck was sure he'd have tried to fire at him again by now. Relaxing just a bit, he continued his story. "I decided to do a perimeter search. Blondie insisted on tagging along."

"Blondie?" Marsh cut him a glance. "Just how old is this mystery woman?"

"I have no idea. Maybe early thirties? She didn't have any weapons or an ID. No cash, either. She looked scared to death but couldn't tell me who or what she was running from."

"Is she for real?"

"Who knows? I suspect she's been assaulted, though. Every time I make an abrupt move toward her, she shies away, putting up her arm as if to ward off a blow. And she has a nice-sized goose egg on the back of her head."

"Humph," Marsh grunted.

"I haven't even gotten to the part about being fired upon three times." He gestured to the wooded area ahead. "Or finding the dead guy."

Marsh sighed. "Not another dead body."

He knew Marsh was talking about a case earlier that year where their fellow Ranger Sam Hayward had found a dead body in a plastic garbage bag on the Whistling Creek Ranch owned by Mari Lynch. Well, Mari Hayward now, as the couple had gotten married a few months ago.

"On the bright side, this one isn't in a garbage bag. And I'm a little more worried about the three rounds of gunfire."

"Your Blondie doesn't know anything about how the guy got dead?"

"Nope." Tuck thought again about the blood staining

her clothes. "Although I'm pretty sure she knows she killed him. She grew upset when I mentioned calling the Diamond County Sheriff's Department. She's worried she'll end up in jail."

"And what do you think?" Marsh cast him a sidelong glance.

"I think the blood on her clothes will match that of the dead guy." He couldn't imagine another scenario. "If she could remember what happened, the guy's death could be ruled as self-defense."

"That's interesting," Marsh scanned the area. "You'd think if she was faking, she'd drop the pretense to avoid being tossed in the slammer."

"Exactly." When they reached the woods, he slowed his pace. "Stay alert. The gunman could be hanging around."

"Yep." Marsh glanced around. "How far is the dead guy?"

"Fifty yards up ahead, give or take a few." Tucker swept his flashlight over the wooded area without seeing the dark shape of the dead body. "We'll run right into him by following the trail of broken branches and crushed leaves left by Blondie's panicked run from the scene of the crime."

Marsh hung back, allowing Tucker to take the lead. "Where is Blondie now?"

"In the house." He didn't mention that he'd given her a shotgun for protection.

"How do you know she'll be there when we're finished out here? Maybe she'll take off."

"She won't get far without a phone, ID or cash. I guess she could pawn her cross necklace, but I don't think so." He'd given her Pops's phone, but there wasn't a rideshare app on the device. Even if there was, there weren't such amenities out here.

"If you say so."

Tucker frowned as they moved farther into the woods. He'd been critical of Blondie not remembering her own name, but here he was, having trouble remembering where the dead body was.

"You mentioned a cross necklace?"

"Yes, and she prays, too." Tucker stopped and swept his flashlight over the woods again. Had he gotten offtrack? Followed the wrong trail? For all he knew, Blondie could have taken a circuitous route to get to the ranch house.

But no, she'd claimed the light from Pops's window had been a beacon drawing her forward.

"Hold up." He lifted a hand to keep Marsh from getting too close. "I may have taken a wrong turn."

"Maybe we should split up?" Marsh suggested.

"Not yet." Tucker took a moment to double-check his location.

With careful deliberation, he inched the beam of his flashlight over the uneven terrain. There was no sign of the dark shape he'd seen earlier.

If he hadn't approached the dead man, checked for a pulse and seen the knife protruding from his gut for himself, Tuck would think he was losing his mind.

A flattened area caught his attention. Keeping the beam of his flashlight on that spot, he quickly crossed through the woods to reach the area.

A few dark blobs of congealed blood covering the ground were all that was left of the dead guy. There was no sign of the body itself.

"What in the world?" he muttered, going down on his haunches to examine the earth more closely. Moving his flashlight, he could see another flattened area just beyond the bloodstained ground.

As if someone had dragged the body.

Marsh came up behind him. "What's wrong?"

Tuck slowly rose to his feet, shaking his head in disbelief. This couldn't be happening. "Looks like someone removed the body."

"Who would do that? And why?"

"I don't know." He sounded just as confused as Blondie had been when he'd point-blank asked her if she'd killed the guy. He squashed a spurt of sympathy as he surveyed the situation.

Other than the blood staining the ground, there wasn't evidence of a crime. Sure, they could still match the blood here to the stains on her clothing, but that didn't mean much. No detective would want to arrest or attempt to convict her of killing a man when there was no body.

The only explanation was that the shooter had removed the dead guy. Or the shooter's accomplice.

But why?

That part didn't make sense.

Unless Blondie was involved in something criminal and her partners in crime were cleaning up after her, to minimize the possibility of her being arrested. If that was the case, the gunfire had been nothing more than a diversion. One used to draw him away from the body so that it could be hauled away.

He looked back at Marsh, who was critically eyeing the dark bloodstains. Then his buddy took an evidence bag from his pocket and picked up several fallen leaves stained with blood.

The local sheriff deputies would arrive any minute.

And frankly, Tuck had no idea what to tell them.

THREE

She awoke with a start, heart pounding as she looked around in confusion. There was a shotgun resting across her lap, and it took a few minutes to remember she'd sought refuge in the ranch house.

And that Tucker Powell had told her to watch over his grandfather.

She hadn't intended to fall asleep, but the sofa was extremely comfortable. Rubbing the back of her head, she tried to remember what had happened.

Leanne.

The name flitted through her mind, making her frown. Leanne? Was that her name? Or maybe a sister's or mother's name?

"Leanne." She said the name out loud, hoping more memories would follow. But they didn't. Swirling red-and-blue lights caught her attention through the window.

The police. She shivered, a wave of apprehension washing over her. Tucker had mentioned calling the police. She sighed, gingerly setting the shotgun aside to stand on shaky knees. She knew that they were here because of the dead man. Well, that and the gunshots, but mostly because of the victim they'd found in the woods.

The man she'd likely killed, despite having no memory of doing such a thing.

There must have been a reason. Yet her mind refused to provide the necessary details of what had transpired. She forced herself to cross the living room toward the window overlooking the front yard.

She could do this. Maybe they wouldn't arrest her on the spot. Maybe they'd take the fact that she was here without money or ID as evidence of being a victim, rather than the perpetrator of the crime.

Please Lord Jesus, enlighten me to the truth!

As she reached the window, she froze as a burly cop slid out from behind the wheel, taking a moment to hitch his pants up. An icy pit of fear settled in her stomach. She ducked and cowered behind the wall, so he wouldn't see her.

Who was he? Had she seen him before? Or was it just that his uniform represented something terrifying?

She pressed a hand to her heart, willing her pulse to settle as she pushed to remember. There was something just out of reach, but what?

Why wouldn't her brain allow her to remember?

Biting down on her lower lip, she considered her options. Her first inclination was to run away, slipping out the bedroom window into the darkness. Yet she feared the police would simply surround the ranch, searching until they found her.

Frozen by indecision, she heard the low murmur of male voices outside. Tucker and his buddy—what was his name? Marsh? They must be talking to the deputies.

She needed to do something.

She pushed away from the wall, then tiptoed through the kitchen toward the hallway. After listening for a moment outside Tucker's grandfather's room, she continued to the room Tucker had offered.

His sister's room.

Her name was Stacy. At least she could remember recent things. She moved to the window and peered out into the darkness. This part of the house overlooked what appeared to be a large barn or stable.

Logically, she assumed it housed animals, like cows and horses. Somehow, she didn't think she had much experience with farm animals, but at this point, she didn't fear them as much as she did the men in uniform talking to Tucker and Marsh.

With resolute determination, she lifted the window. Then she carefully opened the screen as well. She threw one leg over the sill, but paused when she heard voices coming from outside.

"I'm sorry to have bothered you." Tucker's low voice was easily recognizable. "I found a small patch of blood, but that's about all."

Wait, what did he say? A patch of blood? Nothing else?

What about the dead guy?

She swung her leg back into the room and strained to listen.

"I figure I'll send the blood for testing," Tucker said. "We'll wait to get the results back to see if it's animal or human blood. I'll keep you updated on what we find."

"Are you sure you don't want us to spread out and search the property?" a gruff voice asked.

"Ranger Marshall Branson and I have done that, without success," Tucker replied. "This is my grandfather's ranch, so I know the property well. I'm sure you guys have better things to do."

There was a long silence before the gruff voice spoke again. "Okay, then. You'all have a good night."

"You too, Deputy Flores."

She hovered at the window, trying to understand what had just happened. Apparently, Tucker had changed his mind about reporting the dead man. Why, she couldn't fathom.

When she heard a car door slamming shut and a car engine roaring to life, she closed the screen and the window.

Even though the local authorities were leaving, she didn't think she was home free. No, quite the opposite. She expected to be grilled once again by Tucker and his pal Marshall.

If only she could remember.

She'd hoped her memory would return after she'd gotten some rest, but her brief nap on the sofa hadn't helped.

Although the name *Leanne* had flashed in her mind. She decided that was a step in the right direction. Maybe she was Leanne, and this was the beginning of her memory returning. She could hope and pray that after a good night's sleep, the rest of her memories would come back, as well.

Leanne. She tested the name in her mind again as she returned to the kitchen and living room. It didn't seem completely foreign, and was much better than *Blondie*.

"There you are." Tucker's drawl stopped her in her tracks. She hadn't realized the two men had come inside.

"Yes." Eyeing them warily, she tried to smile. "What's going on? Did you talk to the police?"

"We did." Tucker stepped closer, his gaze boring into hers. "They're gone. For now."

The qualification was ominous. There was no mistaking his meaning. The local police would be called back in a nanosecond if necessary.

"Okay." She slid onto the closest stool, more because she needed something solid beneath her. "Why don't you tell me what's going on? I don't understand why they'd leave without taking the dead guy with them."

"Well, that's the thing, Blondie," Tucker drawled. "The dead guy is gone."

"Gone?" She swallowed hard. "I don't understand."

"Your accomplices must have snagged him after using the gunfire as a diversion." Tucker's tone was conversational, but his green gaze smoldered with anger. "It's time for you to come clean. Tell us what's going on, and we will do our best to help."

For some odd reason, it hurt that he'd gone back to treating her as a suspect. "I told you, I don't know what happened to me. Or that man who was stabbed."

"I think your accomplice fired those shots to scare us away from the dead guy, so that he could cover up the crime by sneaking the dead body away."

Was he serious? She lifted her chin. "That's the most ridiculous thing I've ever heard. If I had accomplices, I wouldn't have come running to your house seeking shelter. You said yourself, I was the target of the gunfire, not you!" She belatedly realized she was practically shouting at him, and did her best to lower her voice so she wouldn't wake his grandfather. "I did not set this up. I don't know what's going on or who moved the dead man. But it wasn't me. I'm not involved in this."

"We have a set of bloodstained clothes that proves otherwise," Tucker said. "You all are definitely involved."

"You're right." She flushed, realizing she'd almost forgotten about that pesky detail. She tucked a strand of hair behind her ear. "I know that I'm in danger. Something bad happened that sent me running through the woods to your house. I wish I could tell you what that was, but I can't."

"So you say," Tucker pointed out.

She bit back a sharp retort. Angering her rescuer wouldn't help. She strove for patience. "I know it sounds like something out of Hollywood, but I wish I could remember. Do you think it's easy to walk around in a fog? To not know anything about who I am? Or what happened to me?" She fingered the large bump on her head. "It's not. I feel as if I am walking through a field of buried land mines. One wrong step and I'll blow up."

Tucker continued to glare at her, then glanced at Marshall as if asking his opinion.

"It's late." Marshall shrugged. "Maybe she'll feel better after getting some sleep."

She frowned. "I'm right here."

"Yeah, we see you, Blondie," Tucker said. "You're sure you don't remember anything?"

The way he called her Blondie got on her nerves. Yet, she wasn't sure she wanted to mention how she'd remembered the name *Leanne*. That would open another round of accusations, as if the skeptical expressions on their faces didn't speak volumes already.

"I'm sorry. I wish I did." She slid off the stool. "If you don't mind, I'm going to try to get some sleep."

"You do that." Tucker nodded. "We'll discuss this in more detail tomorrow morning."

We? As in, Marshall was sticking around? She supposed that made sense, considering there was a gunman on the loose. And really, what did it matter? Better two Rangers than the local cops.

"Good night." She turned and walked back to the bedroom, and closed the door behind her. Then she leaned against the wooden door, her thoughts whirling.

What would happen if her memory didn't return? Would Tucker turn her over to the authorities, washing his hands of her?

The idea filled her with dread. Deep down, she felt certain she was safer with Tucker and Marshall than with the local police.

She pushed away from the door, and crawled into bed, pulling the blanket up to her chin. Closing her eyes, she prayed with all her heart that her memory would return.

"I hope you know what you're doing." Marsh lifted a brow.

Yeah, Tuck hoped so, too. "We're law enforcement, right? We can investigate this thing ourselves before handing it over to the locals."

"We absolutely can." Marsh nodded. "The question is whether or not we *should*."

That was the kicker. Tuck raked a hand through his hair, wrestling with his conscience. "We'll get the bloody clothes to the lab tomorrow, along with that sample you took from the woods. From there, we'll figure out our next steps."

"Suit yourself." Marsh yawned. "I'll bunk in your guest room, if you don't mind."

"That works." The ranch house had four bedrooms, more than enough to accommodate them all. Yet, Tucker intended to sleep on the sofa. He didn't expect Blondie to sneak out in the early morning hour, but he figured it was better to be safe than sorry.

Besides, being in the living room would make it easier for him to keep an eye on Pops. Even prior to his grandfather's hip fracture, the older man had been an early riser.

He moved the shotgun from the sofa, somewhat surprised Blondie hadn't kept it close. Considering she claimed to be on the run from danger, he'd figured she'd hang onto the weapon. Especially after she'd checked it like a pro. Her movements had screamed familiarity with guns, and he really wished he understood what was going on.

A woman involved in criminal activity would want to keep the shotgun.

But she hadn't. It irked him that Blondie's actions weren't logical.

He set his service weapon on the end table, well within reach, then stretched out. He hadn't expected to fall asleep, but it seemed like just a few minutes later that he heard a thumping sound.

Tuck shot off the sofa, his gaze zeroing in on his grandfather's door. But then he saw Blondie glancing at him over her shoulder.

"Sorry to wake you." She looked chagrined. "I was planning to make coffee."

"You like coffee?" He inwardly winced at the somewhat accusatory tone.

"I—doesn't everyone?" She frowned. "I don't think knowing you like something is the same thing as remembering."

"Are you telling me you don't remember anything more?" He eyed her curiously.

"Nothing useful." She looked down at her hands for a moment, then up at him. "The name *Leanne* keeps popping into my mind. Either that's my name or someone I care about is named Leanne."

"Leanne, huh?" He couldn't help but wonder if she was making that up.

"Yes. I—uh, thought maybe we could do a search on

missing persons with the name *Leanne*." She grimaced. "It might point us in the right direction."

He had to admit it was a good idea. Unless she was setting him up again. He scrubbed his hands over his face, then rose to his feet. He reached for his weapon, securing the .38 to his belt holster. "Help yourself to coffee. I need to check on Pops."

"Thanks." Blondie—or was it Leanne?—opened another cupboard and managed to find the ground coffee and filters.

Shaking his head, he headed to his grandfather's room. The older man needed help getting around, but was otherwise able to care for himself. He and Stacy didn't want him to fall or hurt himself again, so they'd insisted on taking turns watching over him.

As he helped Pops to the bathroom, Tucker realized he might need Stacy to take over as their grandfather's caregiver. If, as he suspected, the blood on Blondie's shirt matched that of the blood from the now-missing dead guy, he'd have little choice but to head back to the Diamond County Sheriff's Department to get them involved.

Especially since Blondie claimed she still didn't remember anything useful.

Other than she liked coffee.

"We still have a houseguest, huh?" Pops gave him a sly smile. "Good for you. She's pretty."

More like beautiful, but he wasn't about to admit it. Beauty was only skin-deep. He didn't trust her one bit. He decided to go with the name of Leanne, rather than explaining about her amnesia. "Leanne is making coffee, if you're interested. I'll take care of the livestock before breakfast."

"Sounds good to me." Pops leaned heavily on his cane as he led the way out of his room. Tucker and Stacy had tried to get him to use the walker, but the old man had stubbornly refused.

"Good morning." Blondie—er, Leanne—greeted his grandfather with a smile. "Coffee will be ready soon."

Tuck forced a smile. "Leanne, this is my grandfather, Hank Powell. Pops, this is Leanne."

"Nice to meet you, Leanne. Just call me Pops. Everybody else does."

Marsh came down the hall to the kitchen, giving Tucker a questioning look. When Tuck shook his head, Marsh shrugged. "Morning."

"I was just introducing Leanne to Pops," Tuck said. "I need to head out to do the chores, but can make breakfast when I get back."

"I'll help." Marsh's offer made him smile. Tuck was the only one of his fellow Rangers who'd spent significant time as a youngster on a ranch. Sam, Marsh and Jackson had not. Still, he appreciated the offer.

"No need. You can keep an eye on things here." He gave a subtle nod toward Leanne.

"Okay, we'll make breakfast," Marsh said.

Tucker nodded, and left through the mudroom, grabbing his hat on the way out. He strode to the barn and jumped right into the chores, starting with feeding the horses and mucking stalls. The mundane routine gave him way too much time to think about Leanne and the upcoming trip to the lab with the blood samples.

Maybe he and Marsh should take another look around, just to make sure the dead guy hadn't been dragged and dropped in a different location. One that was still part of the Rocking T Ranch.

Leaning on the pitchfork, he used his phone to send Stacy a quick text, asking her to head out as soon as possible and promising to take an extra week off her hands at some point in the future. Thankfully, she didn't protest but responded quickly with an okay emoji.

His sister had more flexibility, as she was able to do her job remotely. Still, she was recently married and wanted to start a family. This juggling of their responsibilities reinforced a truth he and Stacy had been trying to avoid.

Pops needed different living arrangements, and soon.

Tuck was so lost in his troubled thoughts that it took a moment for him to register the scuffling sound seconds before the crack of a gunshot rang out.

His cowboy hat flew off his head beneath the impact of a bullet. Dropping the pitchfork, Tuck pulled out his weapon and ducked behind the stall, even as the mare reared and whinnied loudly to show her displeasure.

He mentally kicked himself for dropping his guard—he should have searched the barn again prior to starting the chores. Now, this guy had him pinned down.

Another gunshot interrupted his self-recriminatory thoughts. Tuck seethed with anger at the way this guy recklessly fired at him, without caring if he hit one of the horses.

He waited a beat, then lifted his head to peer over the top of the stall. Catching movement in the back of the barn, he fired three times in rapid succession. He thought he heard the guy cry out in pain, but then there was nothing but the sounds of the animals, shifting and neighing in the stalls.

A shiver of morning light made him realize the tack door was hanging open. The perp was getting away! Tucker jumped out from the stall and broke into a run.

Bolting from the barn, he saw what appeared to be a man dressed in dark clothing disappearing into the woods. He took off after him, hoping the sound of gunfire had reached Marsh inside the house.

He needed backup!

The man dodged through the trees with a familiarity that boggled Tucker's mind. Had this guy been hiding out here under his nose all night?

Tuck did his best to close the gap, but the suspect had had a head start. After what seemed like eons, Tucker heard the roar of a car engine followed by the squeal of tires.

When he emerged from the other side of the woods, a black pickup truck bounced along the old dirt service road that Pops probably hadn't used in at least ten years, maybe more.

Watching the cloud of dust as the truck disappeared made him grit his teeth in frustration. This guy never should have gotten away.

Then a thought hit hard, and he turned to scan the open area beyond the woods. Yep, there was a stretch of flattened grass, indicating something heavy had been dragged away.

Not only had the shooter escaped last night, taking the dead guy with him, but he'd come back to finish the job.

Tuck thought about Blondie, or Leanne or whatever her name was. He needed answers, and quick.

Before this guy tried again.

FOUR

"Was that gunfire?" Leanne instinctively moved closer to Pops. The older man had jerked his head up, his expression grim.

Marshall had pulled out his own weapon and was moving toward the mudroom door. Leanne scanned the room for the shotgun, glad to know Marshall was heading out to back up Tucker.

Seeing the shotgun propped against the wall, she darted over to grab it. Marsh locked gazes with her for a moment, then nodded as if he agreed with her plan to keep the gun handy to protect herself and Pops.

Then Marsh was gone.

"What's going on?" Pops demanded, sounding cranky. "Did you bring danger to the ranch?"

She hesitated, unsure of how to answer. "I guess so," she finally said. "I'm sorry. I didn't mean to."

The old man's sharp green eyes pierced hers. "Good thing my grandson and his pal are Rangers."

"Yes, I'm very relieved to have their protection." Holding the shotgun with the muzzle pointing at the floor, she moved to the window overlooking the driveway. The same window where she'd glimpsed the cop last night.

Seeing nothing but Marsh's SUV, she moved onto the

next window, the small one over the kitchen sink. The view from this angle was a corner of the barn and part of the corral. Her stomach clenched when she caught a hint of movement, but then quickly recognized Marsh.

Where was Tucker? Was he hit? Her stomach knotted painfully as she sent up a silent prayer.

Please keep Tucker safe in Your care!

"Something's burning," Pops said.

She jerked her attention to the bacon that now appeared extra crispy. She twisted the knob of the stove and grabbed a hot pad to move the skillet. "Sorry about that."

"See anything suspicious?"

She flashed Pops what she hoped was a reassuring smile. "Nope. I'm sure the guys have the situation well under control."

He nodded, but she sensed he was on edge. And she couldn't blame him. The gunfire had sounded close.

Too close.

Unable to settle down, she moved onto the next window, and swept her gaze over the backyard. Seeing nothing out of the ordinary, she headed down the hall to check the windows in each of the four bedrooms. Satisfied that they were relatively safe inside the ranch house, she returned to the kitchen.

Pops had remained at the breakfast counter, sipping his coffee as if there wasn't a gunman on the loose. She tried not to imagine the worst—that Tucker was injured—when she caught a glimpse of two men walking up toward the corral. Her fingers tightened on the shotgun for a moment until she recognized Tucker and Marshall.

Relief weakened her knees. Safe. Tucker was safe. *Thank You, Lord Jesus!*

"Who's out there?" Pops asked gruffly. She caught him

squinting at the window, and could tell he didn't recognize them.

"Tucker and Marsh. They're fine. Looks like they're heading back inside."

"Good," Pops grunted. "I sure hope Tucker took down whoever was doing the shooting."

She blanched at the thought. Yes, Tucker and Marshall were Texas Rangers and had likely been in difficult and dangerous situations before, but this was her fault. She was the one who'd brought a gunman to the ranch.

She glanced down at herself, remembering the bloodstained clothes. She'd been involved in a crime. Either as a witness, victim or perpetrator.

Hopefully not the perpetrator, but to be fair, anything was possible. She didn't want to believe it, but the blood told a disturbing story. The pounding in her head increased when she tried to remember.

She'd had high hopes that her memory would return by morning, but that hadn't happened. How long would it take? Maybe she needed to be seen by a doctor.

The sound of a door opening had her spinning toward the mudroom, bringing the shotgun up as if to take out the threat.

"He drove away in a black pickup truck," Tucker said in a disgusted tone. Letting out a soundless sigh, she lowered the shotgun. "I was too far away to get a plate number, if there even was one. Guy had some nerve, firing at me in the barn where he may have wounded one of the horses."

"Looks like he got too close for comfort," Marsh drawled.

"Yep." Tucker tossed his hat on the breakfast bar. Leanne gasped when she saw the bullet hole piercing the tall crown. "Good thing I had my head tipped down or I'd be toast."

"Did you get him?"

"No, Pops." Tucker's expression softened when he looked at his grandfather. "I followed him across the property, but he had a vehicle out on the old service road."

"Humph. I was hoping you'd have nailed his hide to the barn wall."

The corner of Marsh's mouth quirked up in a grin. "Maybe next time, Pops."

Tucker grimaced and gestured toward the bacon. "I know the gunman left the property, so it's safe enough to finish breakfast. But then we'll need to get out of here." He leveled a glance at his grandfather. "Including you."

"This is my home," Pops protested. "I oughta be able to stay in my own home."

"Do you really want Stacy in danger?" Tucker asked. "I texted to ask her to come out here, but I'm thinking it might be safer for me to take you to her place."

"Bah." Pops waved a hand. "We'll be fine here. We have the livestock to care for."

Tucker sighed loudly, clearly frustrated. Tearing her gaze from the bullet hole in Tucker's hat, she moved to the stove to finish making scrambled eggs. No matter who won this argument, they had to eat.

But if anyone asked her opinion, she agreed with Tucker. The gunman seemed to have made himself at home on the Rocking T Ranch. So much so that she wasn't convinced he'd ever left, despite the way Tucker and Marsh had searched the area. She had no doubt there were many places for someone to hide.

The bullet hole in Tucker's cowboy hat was burned into her memory. He'd barely escaped being shot and killed. The realization shook her to the core. Despite the way Tucker viewed her with blatant suspicion, she abhorred the idea of his being hurt or killed.

For some reason, she felt certain she could trust Tucker, Marsh, and Pops but not anyone else. Especially not local law enforcement.

She needed the two Texas Rangers to help figure out what had taken place to cause her memory loss and send her running to the ranch covered in blood.

"I'll stay on at the Rocking T with Stacy and Pops," Marsh offered. "We can ask Sam and Jackson to meet up with you at the lab when you drop off the blood samples."

Tucker paused in the act of calling his sister. "Are you sure?"

Marsh nodded. "I suspect the danger won't be a factor here for long."

Tuck understood what Marsh was really saying. Leanne was the target, not his grandfather. This had all started with Leanne, and her memory loss was only complicating things. Yes, he'd been under fire in the barn, but it was rather obvious the gunman had attempted to take him out of the picture so that he could get to Leanne.

Removing Leanne from the ranch was probably the best way to keep Pops and Stacy safe.

"Breakfast is ready," Leanne announced.

He hesitated, then nodded at Marsh. "Okay. That works. I'll call Sam and Jackson."

"After we eat," Marsh said. "Heading all the way to the state crime lab in Austin will take several hours. Good thing I happened to be in San Antonio last night."

He nodded, and quickly joined Pops at the breakfast bar. There was just enough room for the four of them to sit and eat.

"I'd like to say grace." Without waiting for a response, Leanne bowed her head. "Lord Jesus, we ask You to bless this food we are about to eat and to keep us all safe in Your care. Amen."

"Amen," he and Marsh echoed. They'd gotten used to praying before meals, now that Sam was a believer. He and Mari had gotten married back in February, and Sam had moved to the Whistling Creek Ranch where Mari lived.

Funny how Sam had become a rancher by default, Tucker thought with a grin.

"Thank you, Leanne," Pops said gruffly. "Your prayer was just what I needed to hear."

"I'm glad." Leanne reached over to gently squeeze his grandfather's hand. Then she quickly passed a large bowl of scrambled eggs, followed by a platter of extra crispy bacon. His grandfather dug into his meal with gusto, which made Tucker feel a little better about the situation.

Surely with Marsh here keeping an eye on things, Pops and Stacy would be fine.

When breakfast was finished, Tucker went back outside to finish the chores. He searched the barn first, then went to work without lingering. Normally, he'd take the horses out for a ride, but this time he simply let them out in the corral. He headed back inside the ranch house.

"Are we really going to Austin?" Leanne asked as she finished drying the dishes. He had to give her credit for pitching in to help. She'd cooked and washed dishes without complaint.

Then again, that's exactly what she would do if she was putting on an act for his benefit.

"Yeah." Her earlier comment about his theory of her involvement being ridiculous had stung. In part, because she was right. It didn't make sense that she would have an accomplice hanging around outside the house to fire at them as a diversion.

But that didn't mean he was willing to let her off the hook. She was involved in this up to her pretty neck. And that would be verified once the lab matched the blood on her clothes with that of the blood found at the scene of the missing dead body.

"Okay." Leanne draped the damp towel over the handle of the oven, then turned to face him. "I'm ready."

Again, her willingness to go along with the plan caught him off guard. She wasn't acting the least bit guilty, and he couldn't decide if that was a good thing or not. He glanced at Marsh, who waved them off.

"We'll be fine." Marsh waved a hand. "But watch your back."

"Thanks." He went down the hall to his room to fetch the two evidence bags. He also took a moment to toss some clothes and toiletries in a duffel bag. No point in coming back to the ranch. It was probably better to stay in town.

Upon returning to the kitchen, he set the bags on the floor by the mudroom as he turned toward Leanne. "You might want to pack a change of clothes, too."

"Are you sure?" She looked doubtful.

"Better to grab some things here so we don't need to stop later."

That worked. She nodded and headed down to his sister's room. She returned a few minutes later.

He gave his grandfather a one-armed hug before walking into the mudroom. He grabbed a spare cowboy hat, preferring one that didn't have a bullet hole in the felt. The weather was still warm enough that Leanne shouldn't need a coat, but he grabbed Stacy's wool-lined fleece. "Here, keep this in case the weather changes."

"Thanks." She draped it over her arm. "I hope I get a chance to thank your sister, too."

As he intended to keep Blondie far away from Stacy, he didn't respond. He opened the door, looked around, then gestured for Blondie—Leanne, he silently corrected—to follow.

His SUV was in the garage next to his grandfather's pickup truck. There was more than enough room to maneuver around Marsh's vehicle. As he left the Rocking T Ranch, Tucker tried to relax. It wasn't easy, because even though he was confident Marsh would protect his family, he still didn't know much more about what was going on than he had last night. He glanced at Leanne, noting her drawn features. "How's your head?"

"Still hurts. Not as bad as last night."

"After we drop the evidence at the state lab in Austin, I'll take you to the hospital." He should have taken her to the clinic to be examined last night. "I'm sure the doc will want to do a CT scan of your brain."

She fingered the bump on the back of her head. "I'm fine. I'm sure I'd feel much worse and have additional symptoms if there was any internal bleeding."

He shrugged. He wasn't a medical expert, and that was the point. Better to have a doctor clear her.

As he drove, he kept an eye on the rearview mirror. There wasn't a lot of traffic on the highway behind him, but that was partially because his grandfather's ranch stretched for several miles.

The closer they got to San Antonio, and then Austin, the more difficult it would be to catch someone tailing them.

"I would like to ask a favor," Leanne said, breaking the silence.

He arched a brow. "Oh, yeah?"

She flushed and stared down at her hands for a moment. "If you have to arrest me, I would prefer you take me into federal custody."

Of all the favors he'd expected to hear, that was not one of them. "Why on earth would you want to be taken into federal custody?"

"I don't know." She sighed loudly. "I told you I don't remember. I just have a feeling that I can't trust anyone other than you and Marsh. If I have to go to jail…" Her voice trailed off.

He frowned. "If you trust me, then tell me what happened."

"I would if I could," she snapped, then sighed again. "Please, Tucker. Don't leave me with the local police."

His vehicle ate up the miles as he considered her odd request. As a cop, he'd learned to trust his instincts. If he could bring himself to believe in her innocence, he would tell her to trust her instincts, too. "Reckless homicide or assault with a deadly weapon isn't a federal crime."

"I don't care. Make something up." She threw up her hands in exasperation. "I would rather you didn't arrest me at all! I don't think this is an unreasonable request."

This was a first. He'd never had anyone ask to be taken into custody. Then again, he'd never been in a situation like this, either. He finally nodded. "Okay, I will arrest you on federal charges if necessary."

"Thank you." She turned to stare out the window, making him feel like a jerk for being difficult.

They drove in silence for the next two hours. Leanne rested, which was a good thing. As predicted, traffic picked up as they drew closer to Austin. He noticed a black pickup truck hanging back several car lengths behind him. He began to vary his speed, going faster for ten minutes, then slowing down.

The driver of the vehicle never closed the gap between them.

The problem with shaking a tail in Texas was that there weren't enough intersections with highways and streets available to use in an evading tactic. If he'd have seen the guy sooner, near San Antonio, he could have lost him. But this stretch of highway wasn't busy at all.

"Call Jackson," he said to activate the call.

The other end of the line rang three times before his fellow Ranger answered. "What's up, Tuck?"

"We're thirty minutes outside of Austin, and I picked up a tail." Leanne's head snapped around to look at him. "I may need your help."

"I'm in Austin, not that far from the Capitol building," Jackson said. "Do you want me to head out to meet you?"

"Yes." He pressed on the accelerator, picking up speed. As before, the vehicle behind him did the same. "I don't like this, so you'd better hurry."

"Call the state patrol," Jackson advised. "I'll be there as soon as I can."

"Thanks." He ended the call, knowing he needed to stay focused. He pressed another key to bring up a GPS map. As he glanced at the streets where he could try to make an abrupt turn, it occurred to him that the driver in the vehicle behind him could have the same advantage.

Not good.

He didn't want to head too far from Austin, where there were plenty of local cops to offer backup. Eyeing the vehicle in the rearview mirror, he thought it seemed to be getting closer.

Sensing the driver was about to make his move, he decided he was running out of time. There was no way for him to get to Austin.

And if that wasn't an option, then he needed a plan B. He punched the gas. Leanne gasped and clung to the door handle. As they approached the next intersection, the only one available within the next five miles, he waited until the last possible minute to hit the brake and crank the wheel. The tires of his SUV squealed in protest. After making the turn, he floored the gas pedal again, hoping to outmaneuver the driver behind him.

A quick glance in the rearview mirror proved he hadn't. The good news was that the black truck had fallen at least half a mile behind them. The bad news was that the driver hadn't given up the chase.

"Tucker?" Leanne's voice was thick with fear. "What's happening? Where are we going?"

"Anywhere we can ditch the guy behind us." He didn't look at her, because there was a car up ahead of them. A silver pickup truck.

One that was moving slower than usual. Texans were not known for obeying speed limits.

His gut clenched. An older driver? Or a trap?

"Keep your head down." They bore down on the silver truck. There wasn't much of a shoulder on either side of the road, but what little space that was available would have to do.

They were fresh out of options.

He prayed the driver was an older person, like his grandfather, who wasn't in a hurry to reach his or her destination. Gripping the wheel tightly, he abruptly swerved off the road to go around the slow silver truck, illegally passing him on the right. He glanced quickly at the driver at the exact same time the driver looked at him. Their gazes clashed and held for a long second.

Then the driver raised a gun, pointing the barrel right at him.

Tucker belatedly realized the passenger's side window of the silver truck was open. He ducked his head and punched the gas, praying this wasn't the end of the line.

The sharp retort of gunfire rang out, striking the rear driver's side window and missing his head by less than two inches.

"Tucker!" Leanne cried. "Are you hurt?"

"I'm fine. Stay down!" He didn't dare look over at her, staying focused on passing the silver truck. His wheels spun a bit on the loose gravel along the side of the road, but then he was back on solid ground, doing his best to add more distance between them and the silver truck.

Unfortunately, the driver who'd shot at him wasn't letting go so easily. Despite being a slowpoke on the road earlier, the driver of the silver truck was coming up fast behind them, closing the gap with apparent ease.

Making Tucker realize this had been a trap all along.

One he'd fallen for, hook, line and sinker.

FIVE

Leanne fumbled for Pops's older-model phone Tucker had given her, doing her best to dial 911. It seemed to take forever for the operator to answer.

"This is 911. What's your emergency?"

"Someone is shooting at us!" As she said the words, there was a strange sense of familiarity about them. Had she said them before? "We're heading north on US 59."

"I'll send state troopers to the area," the operator said calmly. "Is anyone hurt?"

"Not yet." Lifting her head, she swept her gaze over Tucker. His expression was grim, but she didn't see any blood. "Please hurry."

"Stay on the line," the operator said.

She was about to reply when the connection came to an abrupt end. She frowned, wondering if they were in a cell tower dead zone when she realized the phone had run out of battery.

It hadn't occurred to her to ask to borrow the charger last night. With a sigh, she dropped the phone in the cup holder of the center console.

"Hang on." Tucker's warning came as he abruptly wrenched the wheel, nearly giving her whiplash.

More gunfire rang out, making her flinch. Cool air streamed through the broken rear window.

How long could they hold the shooter off? She was afraid to ask.

The shrill wail of police sirens brought a mixture of fear and relief. It wasn't logical to be afraid of the local law enforcement agencies, but there was no denying her visceral reaction to the sound and sight of cops.

Not Texas Rangers, though. Which again, didn't make sense.

"He's falling back!" Tucker sounded relieved. Then his frown deepened as he eased on the brake. "I don't want to lose him completely. It would be great if the local cops could grab him."

She sat upright and twisted in the seat. The silver truck was so far back she couldn't see it clearly. "Can you tell which direction the sirens are coming from?"

He shook his head. "Hard to say, the way sound travels out here."

She understood what he meant. There was so much wide-open space between highways that it wasn't easy to pinpoint the location.

"Call Jackson," Tucker said out loud. A moment later, the sound of a phone ringing echoed through the car.

"Tuck, where are you?" Jackson asked.

"We had to bail onto US 59 heading north, but I need you to be on alert for a silver truck. Driver in his midthirties carrying a thirty-eight."

"I was wondering why I couldn't find you. Glad you're okay. I'll keep going for a while yet to see if I can pick up the silver truck. We'll meet back at the state crime lab."

"Sounds good, Jackson."

Leanne was glad that Tucker had his buddies for support. She caught the flicker of red-and-blue lights coming toward them from the north.

She twisted in her seat again to look through the broken window. The silver truck was nothing more than a speck on the road. Thirty seconds later, it disappeared.

Tucker thumped the steering wheel. "They got away."

She could relate to his frustration. Since her memory was nothing but a black hole, they needed to grab one of these bad guys to understand what was going on.

To find out who wanted to kill her, and why.

Tucker pulled off on the side of the road and flipped on his hazard lights. She glanced at him. "What are you doing? We can't sit here and wait for the police. I don't have an ID on me and can't even give them my name or contact information."

He winced. "I'd forgotten about that. You're right." He turned off the lights and pulled back out onto the highway, quickly getting up to the speed limit. "It doesn't seem right to make the emergency call then leave the scene of the crime."

"I'm sorry." She didn't know what else to say. He was right about protocol. A flash of guilt hit hard. Her ending up on his grandfather's ranch was likely putting his career at risk. Yet, just imagining the third degree they'd get when the officers asked for her name and contact information convinced her that leaving was the right decision.

"It's fine." He glanced over as the two squads sped past. "I didn't get the license plate of the silver truck, so issuing a BOLO for the vehicle is pointless. Jackson has the best chance of spotting it, and even that is a long shot."

"Did you recognize the driver?"

He looked thoughtful for a moment. "No, he didn't look familiar. Younger than I anticipated, but I was judging his age by how slow he was driving. That was before I discovered they'd drawn us into a trap."

That possibility hadn't occurred to her. "You really think the drivers of the two trucks were working together?"

"Yeah." He sighed and rubbed his chin. "I think the driver of the black truck hung back until we reached that specific stretch of highway. The silver truck was in position, waiting for us. The driver of the black truck knew that if he came up fast, I'd try to lose him. Going to the right is always easier when implementing an evasion maneuver." He sounded disgusted with himself. "They were one step ahead of us the whole time."

Hearing him describe the sequence of events brought the gunman's plan into focus. "I wonder if they were hiding somewhere along the road leaving the ranch."

"Had to be. I looked but didn't see anything." He shook his head. "But we were set up by a two-man team. The silver truck was stationed several miles ahead of us. The two cars could have been communicating by phone or radio. Either way, the silver truck maintained his position until we caught up to him. Then at the right moment, he shot us."

"Devious."

"Exactly." He glanced at her. "It's crucial that you remember what happened, and soon. Before things spiral further out of control."

"I wish I could." Didn't he understand how difficult this was for her? Not knowing her name, what she did for a living or anything else about herself was awful. Even if she had killed a man in self-defense, she'd rather know exactly what had transpired than be stuck in limbo. "If you want me to be seen at the hospital, I will. I want to know what's going on just as much as you do."

He nodded but didn't say anything more. She hoped that

meant he was starting to believe her. She was sick and tired of defending herself.

He turned left to head west toward Austin. Tucker was forced to slow down as the city came into view. She frowned, struck by a sense of familiarity. She knew that when he took the next turn to the left, the white dome of the state capitol building would come into view.

A chill washed over her. There was no doubt she'd been in Austin before. But when? With whom? And doing what? Did she live there? Work there?

Hide out there?

Which side of the line was she on? That of the good guys—police, firefighters or Rangers, like Tucker?

Or on the wrong side? Had she aligned herself with criminals? Those who existed within the underbelly of society?

She didn't want to believe she was a criminal, but forced herself to keep an open mind.

When Tucker took a side street, doing his best to avoid the congested traffic, an apartment building caught her eye. Her gaze zeroed in on the third-floor corner apartment.

Her place? Or someone else's?

She had no way of knowing. Still, she made a note of the address. Once they'd dropped off the evidence bags at the state crime lab, she'd ask Tucker to drive her back.

A flicker of hope burned in her heart. Maybe being in familiar surroundings would allow her memories to rush back.

Please Lord Jesus, guide us to the truth!

Tucker noticed how Leanne's gaze had clung to the six-story apartment building on the right side of the street. Had she recognized it?

He hated to admit that her memory loss came across

as too real to be faked. He felt certain she'd have slipped up by now if her intent was to play him. Especially since they've been targeted by gunfire four times in less than twelve hours.

His phone rang, startling him. Seeing Jackson's name on the dashboard screen, he quickly answered. "Did you find the truck?"

"Negative. I'm heading back to Austin."

Tuck tried not to be disappointed. "Thanks for trying. We're less than five minutes from the crime lab. We'll wait for you to get here."

"See you soon." Jackson ended the call.

"There are so many pickup trucks on the roads that finding the shooter's vehicle will be impossible without a unique identifier," Leanne said. "A license plate, bumper sticker, college football flag, even dents or dings."

For the first time since she'd climbed in through his grandfather's window, she sounded like a cop. Normal people didn't use terms like *unique identifier*.

"Do you like college football?"

She frowned, then nodded. "Yes, I think I do. Although I don't have any clear memories of attending a game."

He wanted to push for more information, but the state office building came into view up ahead. He focused on navigating the traffic to pull into the parking lot.

"You work out of this building?" Leanne gestured toward it.

"We're deployed around the entire state, but yes, for the most part this serves as our headquarters." He slid out from behind the wheel and headed to the back to retrieve the evidence bags.

Leanne continued to look around with interest as they went inside. The lab was on the ground floor, and the offices, including the one his boss used, were on the upper floors. He gestured to a couple of plastic chairs lined against the wall. "Have a seat. This won't take long."

She grimaced, but didn't argue or try to follow him down the hall. Leaving her alone wasn't easy. He couldn't shake the possibility that she was waiting for the right moment to ditch him.

Thanks to his former girlfriend, trusting women wasn't his strong suit.

The lab was manned by Helen, a cheerful woman in her midsixties. When he dropped the evidence bags on the desk, she smiled. "Sweet Tucker, always bearing gifts."

He had to laugh. "Yeah, these are gifts, all right. I need the blood on clothing in bag number one compared to the blood on the leaves and soil contained in bag number two. I know DNA will take time, but I need whatever can be gleaned from preliminary testing as quickly as possible."

"Of course," Helen said. "Just sign them in, and I'll get them processed right away."

"Thanks." He hesitated. "Have you heard anything about a John Doe being brought to the morgue recently? Like in the past few hours?"

"Not a thing. And usually, a John Doe arrives with other evidence to process, too. Like that." She gestured to the bags. "You might want to stop in to see the medical examiner, though." She grinned. "Could be your John Doe arrived without clothes and personal items."

She was joking, but his thoughts went back to the man who'd been stabbed in the abdomen and left on his ranch property. He'd been wearing clothes. Shoes, too. But the body had been dragged away, presumably by the gunman, so anything was possible.

"I will. Thanks, Helen." He turned away and used his

phone to call the ME's office. The receptionist confirmed that no new unknown males had been brought it. With a sigh, he pocketed his phone and returned to the lobby. A wave of relief washed over him when he saw Leanne sitting in one of the uncomfortable plastic chairs.

She hadn't ditched him. At least, not yet.

"That didn't take long." She rose to her feet.

"No." He glanced at his watch. "It's probably going to take a good twenty minutes for Jackson to get here. Sometimes I forget how bad our early morning traffic can be."

She caught her lower lip between her teeth. "As we came down the street, I noticed a six-story apartment building."

"Oh yeah?" He arched a brow. "Did it look familiar?"

"Yes, in fact it did." She held his gaze for a long moment. "I know you're having trouble believing me, Tucker, but I get the sense I've lived in Austin at some point in my life. I was thinking we should head back to the apartment building and see if being inside sparks any memories."

He nodded thoughtfully. "It can't hurt to try. But I still think we need to get you examined by a doctor."

She shrugged. "I probably should go in, but it occurred to me that being in familiar surroundings may be the best way to spark a memory. And if my memory returns, there's no reason to head to the hospital."

It was hard to argue with her logic. He was no expert, but the fact that Leanne was able to recall recent events and make rational decisions seemed to indicate she did not have a significant head injury.

Although, it would be difficult to forgive himself if she took a sudden turn for the worse.

He reached for his phone. "I'll have Jackson meet us there, instead."

"Great." She looked relieved. "Thank you. This means a lot to me."

He nodded, battling a flash of guilt over the fact he hadn't done anything to warrant her gratitude. Just the opposite. He'd treated her rather badly. Or at least with more suspicion than she'd deserved. He quickly called Jackson to let him know they were going to the apartment building.

"Why the change in plan?"

"Leanne believes the place is familiar. Like she lived there at some point. It's on the way, so just stop there instead."

"Okay. I suppose it doesn't matter where we meet. Traffic is a bear no matter which way I go," his buddy groused.

"See you soon." Tuck ended the call. "Ready?"

"Yes." There was a gleam of anticipation in Leanne's blue eyes, as if she was excited at the prospect of remembering. An unexpected flash of attraction made him take a step toward her, then he hastily caught himself.

What was he doing? How could he be attracted to a woman he didn't trust?

Especially someone who didn't know anything about herself. She could be married, engaged or seeing someone.

Stay focused on the danger, he silently reprimanded himself. She was either a victim or a perp. Not a potential date.

He turned and resolutely headed for the door.

Leanne eagerly fell into step beside him. "I have a good feeling about this," she said as they stepped into the bright sunlight. "Being out on the ranch didn't seem at all familiar. Maybe I'm a city girl at heart."

"Yeah. Maybe." He glanced at her. "But you were someplace close to the ranch for a reason."

"Right." Her expression fell. "I wonder why?"

He opened the car door for her, then slid behind the

wheel. She craned her neck to look around as he retraced their earlier drive to reach the apartment building.

Parking wasn't easy to find, which made him wonder if there was underground parking or if most of the apartment residents walked, rode a bike or took public transit to work each day. As if on cue, a large bus lumbered by.

"There's a spot." Leanne pointed to a reasonable gap between two cars. The street parking was limited to a two-hour time frame, but they wouldn't be there that long.

He parallel parked, then climbed out. Leanne quickly joined him. "See those two windows on the corner of the third floor? I feel like that may be where I lived. Or where someone I was close to lived."

"A boyfriend?" He wasn't sure why he'd asked, since he knew she couldn't remember. He hastily added, "Or a college roommate? Maybe a sibling."

She frowned. "I'm not sure."

They crossed the street and headed toward the main entry. As they approached, two younger women came out of the building, wearing what appeared to be general office attire. He half expected them to recognize Leanne, but they didn't.

Interesting.

He jumped forward to grab the door before it could close, in case it was kept locked.

"Let's go to the third floor," Leanne whispered. She turned and headed up the stairs, ignoring the elevator.

She certainly acted as if she'd lived here, he thought as he followed her up to the third floor. She turned to the left and walked down the hall to the very last apartment, which faced the street where they'd parked.

Apartment 324.

She stood for a moment, staring at the door as if willing herself to remember.

He hung back, watching and waiting. Trying to hide his impatience.

She reached out and tried the door handle. Of course it was locked. After another long ten seconds, she turned away. "Nothing. Other than it looks familiar."

Breaking in seemed drastic, so he gestured back toward the stairwell. "Let's check the mailboxes to find the last name of the occupant."

They took the stairs back down to the main floor. Leanne walked to the row of mailboxes. The box associated with apartment 324 had the name *Wolfe* written in block letters.

"Leanne Wolfe." She tried the name out, as if she were interviewing for a position. Then sighed. "Could be mine, but a first initial would have been helpful."

"We can do a search on the name *Leanne Wolfe*, see if anything pops up." Irrationally, he wanted to make her feel better. "We were planning to do a search on your first name anyway."

"Yes, that should narrow things down. If it's my name," she added. "And if I lived here at some point. I really expected to be hit by a flood of memories, but there's nothing other than a vague sense of familiarity. So vague that it could be that I lived in another apartment building similar to this one."

He masked his disappointment. "No worries. I think it's progress that you even noticed the apartment building." He gestured toward the door. "Let's go outside and wait for Jackson."

He stepped to the side to allow her to go first. She pushed the door open. "Wait, I have an idea." As she turned back toward the mailboxes, a crack of gunfire rang out, shattering the glass door to the apartment building.

Tucker yanked Leanne out of the way with one hand, and pulled his weapon from his holster with the other. He pressed himself against the wall, wondering how the shooter had found them.

Unless the shooter knew more about Leanne than they did. As he peeked around the corner to try to spot the gunman, he grimly realized they may have found the correct apartment building after all.

SIX

Huddling next to Tucker, Leanne wrestled with a flash of anger. When would this nightmare stop? Why did the gunman keep coming after her? Being targeted by these men was getting old.

She really wanted her memory to return.

"Jackson, where are you? We need backup." Tucker spoke in a curt tone. She hadn't even realized he'd called his fellow Ranger. "Get here ASAP!"

She was certain the local police would arrive on scene before Jackson. This wasn't his grandfather's ranch in the middle of nowhere. This was downtown Austin. People didn't shoot each other here.

The wail of sirens confirmed her suspicion.

"Stay back," Tucker warned, and dropped his phone in his pocket then eased around the corner, holding his weapon ready. His muscles were tight, his entire body on full alert. She wanted to reach out and grab his arm to hold him back.

She couldn't bear the idea of something happening to Tucker.

Despite the rush-hour traffic, the police sirens grew louder. Tucker had said to stay back, but she crept forward so she could look out at the street.

To her surprise, a man wearing a cowboy hat and silver

star on his chest was standing and talking to Tucker. Jackson must have gotten there faster than anticipated.

"We need to spread out and search for the shooter," Tucker said.

"We'll need the locals to help with that." Jackson shrugged. "Technically, this is their jurisdiction."

Since there was no sign of the gunman, she stepped over the broken glass littering the ground, and joined the two men. Tucker scowled, but she ignored him, focusing her attention on Jackson. "You got here quick. Did you get any glimpse of the shooter? Or at least where he was standing when he fired at the front door of the apartment building?"

Jackson and Tucker exchanged a pointed glance. "You sound like a cop," Jackson said.

She frowned, trying to imagine herself wearing a police uniform. The image didn't jell in her mind. "I highly doubt that. It's basic common sense to find the location the shooter used to fire his weapon. Especially when there's the chance that he may have left shell casings behind."

They exchanged another long look. "I'll head out to scout the area," Jackson said when Tucker remained silent. "You'all need to fill in the local police on what's happening."

The thought of doing that brought a wave of dread. She grabbed Tucker's arm. "Maybe we should go."

"It's too late for that." Tucker nodded to the squad cars that were already double-parking in the street. "I'll call my boss, see if he can help pull rank."

She bit her lip, wishing she could go back in time. She'd thought coming here to the apartment building would be a surefire way for her memory to return.

Instead, they'd walked right into danger.

And how had the gunman known to find them there?

Before she could delve into that, two sets of Austin police officers came striding toward them.

And so it begins, she thought grimly.

"Officers, I'm Texas Ranger Tucker Powell, and this Leanne, a witness under my protection." She shouldn't have been surprised Tucker took the lead. "My partner Jackson Woodlow has begun searching the area for the shooter."

"What happened?" The question came from the only female officer of the group.

"We were checking out the apartment building when someone fired at the front door." Tucker's phone rang, so he pulled it from his pocket. "Excuse me. This is my boss."

"Wait a minute. Are you saying this is your case?" the oldest officer of the group asked.

They looked at her, but Leanne had no idea what to say, so she remained silent. Interesting that he'd introduced her as his witness.

Remembering her bloodstained clothes, she wanted to believe that was true. And obviously, he couldn't refer to her as a possible perp.

"Yes, sir," Tucker was saying. "I'll let the local police know."

The older cop groaned. "You're taking the case."

"I'm afraid so," Tucker said. "My boss is reaching out to your sergeant."

The four cops looked extremely disgruntled, but Tucker acted as if he didn't care. He drew Leanne away, his gaze sweeping the area. "Don't say anything to the local police, okay?" he whispered. "The less they know, the better."

"I understand." She glanced back over her shoulder at the four officers. "But what's to prevent them from investigating on their own?"

"Their boss will tell them to stand down. It will work

out." He frowned. "My boss wants to meet with you at some point, but I think our first priority is to get you to safety."

She appreciated his concern. "It's reassuring to know the Rangers are keeping the case," she said in a low voice. "I trust you and Marsh and Jackson over anyone else."

Especially the police. If only she could figure out why she didn't have faith in the local authorities. Even cops from Austin didn't evoke a sense of safety.

He looked as if he wanted to ask more questions, but Jackson jogged toward them. "Found a casing," he said with obvious satisfaction. "I've asked our boss, Owens to send crime-scene techs here to search the inside of the apartment-building lobby for the slug."

"Good," Tucker said. "The more evidence we can compile on this, the better."

"Right." Jackson held up the evidence bag. "I'll drop this at the lab and ask them to put a rush on it."

"They may still be doing the blood analysis I requested," Tucker said. "And that may give us more to go on. When you stop at the lab, grab a laptop for us to use."

"Good idea," Jackson agreed.

"In the meantime, we need a plan for Leanne. Clearly this guy knows her better than we do."

Jackson nodded thoughtfully. "Let's grab a motel on the south side of town. Better to stay there in case we need to get back to your grandfather's ranch for some reason."

"San Antonio would be closer." She remembered how they'd gone around that city on their way to Austin.

"I think we should stay close to Austin."

She nodded at Tucker, even though she knew she wouldn't be safe until she remembered what had transpired the night before.

What had caused her to stab that man.

Was this about revenge? Had she killed some cartel leader? Or some other well-known criminal? And now his guys wanted her to pay the ultimate price?

It was easier to go down that line of thinking rather than to believe she'd killed an innocent man.

As they stood there, she noticed drivers passing by stared at her curiously. A chill snaked down her spine.

For all she knew, one of them could be the shooter.

"There are the crime scene techs." Tucker waved toward the white van that pulled up, then reached for her arm. "Let's go. We'll follow Jackson."

She nodded and allowed him to guide her toward their parked SUV. Minutes later, they were back on the road, pushing their way through the congested traffic.

It seemed wrong to leave the crime scene, yet she was glad to be away from the gawkers. She scanned the faces of the people they passed, hoping someone would look familiar.

Anything to fill the void where her memory was supposed to be.

Tucker pulled into the parking lot of the state building. They watched as Jackson ran inside with the evidence bag in hand. Looking at the clock, she realized a full ninety minutes had passed since they'd been there earlier.

Time flies even when you're not having fun. She sighed.

Jackson quickly returned to his vehicle. After merging back into traffic, she resumed scanning the faces of people driving past.

"Try not to push it." Tucker broke the silence. "Your memory will return soon. And we have a few leads now on how to find you."

She turned to look at him. "You think that was my apartment?"

"Don't you?" Tucker asked. "Why else would the gunman know to show up there?"

He had a point. Was her name Leanne Wolfe? She'd assumed that knowing her name would bring a flood of memories.

It didn't.

And maybe her memory would never return. She turned away, feeling certain her life would never be the same again.

A thought that only dragged her deeper into the dark pit of despair.

Tucker was convinced Blondie was Leanne Wolfe. Having her name was the first step. Soon they'd know exactly what was going on, and why she'd shown up at Rocking T Ranch with a dead man's blood staining her clothes.

His phone rang. Seeing Jackson's name, he quickly answered. "What's wrong?"

"Nothing, but I haven't eaten, and it's close to lunchtime. I'm going to pull into the family restaurant next to the Sun Valley Motel."

"Sounds good. We'll join you for lunch." Normally, Tucker was the one obsessed with food, but he'd been distracted by recent events. "Bring the laptop in with you."

"Will do." Jackson ended the call.

"I'm not very hungry," Leanne said.

"Is your headache worse?" He still felt guilty over not taking Leanne to the hospital. "If so, it's probably best if we head over to the emergency department. I know I should have taken you last night, but better late than never."

"No, thank you," she said politely. "My headache is about the same. And I'd rather not go to the emergency department. For some reason, I don't think it's smart to have my name in the hospital computer system. If *Leanne Wolfe* really is my name."

Based on the way the shooter had shown up at the apartment building, he was inclined to agree. "Okay, but if you change your mind at any point, let me know."

"I won't. But thanks." She put her hand to her temple. "There are no words to explain how frustrating this is. To hear a name like *Leanne Wolfe* but to not recognize it as my own."

She was right. He had no idea what that felt like. "We'll do a search on you. Maybe seeing photographs will help."

"Maybe." She didn't sound convinced.

They drove in silence for several minutes. The traffic thinned as they left the city limits. The restaurant Jackson had in mind was across the street from the motel. They had used the Sun Valley Motel before, and the only downside to the setup was that there was only one way in and out of the rooms.

Securing connecting rooms would help mitigate that concern. But it wasn't the perfect solution. Especially since he couldn't bring himself to fully trust Leanne. She could be a perp rather than a victim.

And if that was the case, once she remembered what had happened—specifically the details surrounding why she'd killed a man—he wouldn't put it past her to slip away in the dead of night. The only reason she needed him now was because she had no money, phone or car.

Not to mention, being constantly stalked by a pair of gunmen.

There was more than one bad guy after them, which made the situation dicey. He was glad Marsh had stayed back to guard Pops and Stacy, but they may need Sam's help, too.

Tucker pulled into the restaurant parking lot behind Jackson. They headed inside, his stomach growling at the commingled scent of tacos, burgers and fries.

"Let's grab a booth," Jackson said.

They waited for the hostess to return. "We'd like to sit there." Tuck nodded toward the empty booth near the restrooms. It was the only empty booth with a direct line of sight to the main entrance.

After the gunfire at the apartment building, he wasn't sitting with his back to another possible point of attack.

"Follow me." The hostess scooped up menus and led the way through the maze of tables.

He gestured for Leanne to slide in first, then essentially blocked her in by sitting beside her. Jackson took the bench across from them.

If Leanne didn't like the arrangement, she didn't let on.

After taking their drink orders—everyone going with sun tea—their server left them to peruse the menus.

"They serve breakfast all day," Jackson said. "That works for me."

"I'll have the chicken sandwich." Leanne pushed her menu aside. "I hate not remembering anything about my past, yet I know I like grilled chicken."

He caught Jackson's wry glance, and understood his buddy was just as skeptical about her amnesia. Ironically, he'd come to believe her memory had been lost. He nodded. "I'm sure it's difficult."

"You mentioned matching the blood from my clothes to that of the dead man." She toyed with her glass of iced tea. "How soon will we know if they match?"

"I was hoping they'd have called me by now," he admitted. "But I think we should operate under the assumption that the blood will match. I think the better question is who dragged him off the ranch?"

Jackson grimaced. "Sounds like someone is covering their tracks."

"I agree." He eyed his friend. "Two gunmen are doing their best to kill Leanne. Makes me mighty curious about who the other victim is."

"I wondered the same thing," Leanne said. "Like maybe I killed some cartel member or some other criminal with subordinates that are seeking revenge on me."

"That's one thought. Or, you were in the wrong place at the wrong time. Maybe you stumbled upon the crime and had to stay back with the dead man while the real culprits took off." He spread his hands. "There are many different scenarios that might explain why the dead guy's blood is on your clothes."

"Nice of you to give me the benefit of the doubt," Leanne said. He glanced at her, expecting to see sarcasm.

But she looked grateful.

Somehow, he managed not to slide his arm around her shoulders in a reassuring hug. Being her protector was messing with his mind. He couldn't afford to let his guard down.

His role as a Texas Ranger meant traveling across the second-largest state in the continental US. His home base being in Austin didn't mean much, since he'd been to every corner of the state. His last girlfriend, Cherry Anderson, had not been able to handle the long absences. When he'd come home early to surprise her, he was the one who'd been shocked right out of his boots.

Cherry had not been alone. She'd been entwined on the sofa with another man. And when he'd caught her red-handed, so to speak, she'd blamed him for her transgression.

Maybe Leanne wasn't a murderer, but she was still off-limits.

Their server returned with their food. He glanced at Leanne, knowing she'd want to say grace.

"Dear Lord Jesus, we thank You for keeping us safe earlier today. We ask for Your blessing as we continue to seek the truth. Amen."

"Amen," he and Jackson echoed.

Jackson added half a bottle of hot sauce to his scrambled eggs and hash browns before digging in. Shaking his head wryly, Tucker took a bite of his burger, pleased that the meat had been prepared medium rare.

Exactly the way he liked it.

"I take it we're staying at the motel across the street?" Leanne eyed them curiously. "I get the feeling you've brought other people here before."

"Yup." He didn't explain further. "But don't be concerned about the arrangements. You'll have plenty of privacy as we'll use connecting rooms."

"I'm not worried." She nibbled on a french fry. "Especially since I don't have the same sense of familiarity here that I had back at the apartment building. This should work fine for keeping me off the grid."

There she went again, sounding just like a cop. Maybe a former police officer? Although she was far too young to be retired.

She'd mentioned drug cartels, so maybe she was with the drug enforcement agency? Or even a local cop from down near the border? All interesting possibilities. He filed them away for later, once he had time to log into the laptop.

If he was honest, he'd admit Leanne being a cop of some sort made more sense than being a criminal. Except that she'd arrived on his grandfather's ranch in street clothes stained with blood. And no ID, gun, phone or cash.

Had she been working an undercover operation that had gone wrong? Maybe.

A phone buzzed. He and Jackson patted their pockets. Jackson pulled his device out. "Hey, Sam," he said, letting Tucker know who he was talking to. "Where are you?"

Tucker couldn't hear the other end of the conversation, but at the frown puckering Jackson's brow, he assumed the news wasn't good.

"Sorry to hear that. Give Mari our love and don't worry. We'll be fine." Jackson lowered the phone. "Sam is taking Mari to the hospital. She's caught a wicked flu bug, and with being four months pregnant, they want to give her IV fluids and keep an eye on her."

"I agree. Sam's place is with his wife and son." Mari's five-year-old son, Theo, wasn't Sam's by blood, but he was the only father the child had ever known. Sam had formally adopted the boy, and Theo called him dad.

Leanne stiffened and grabbed his arm. "Tucker? Do you see them?"

"Who?" He nonchalantly turned to scan the restaurant. Then he understood. "The sheriff's deputies?"

"Yes." Her voice had dropped to a whisper. "I can see by their patches on their uniforms that they're from Diamond County." Her fingers tightened. "That's where the Rocking T Ranch is located."

He nodded in understanding. "You're wondering what they're doing way out here."

"Yes." She leaned back in the booth so that his body would shield her from view. "This restaurant isn't anywhere close to their jurisdiction."

She had a good point. He glanced at Jackson, who was also frowning.

"They're giving me a bad feeling," Leanne murmured. "I don't want them to see me."

They were just about finished, so Tucker pulled money from his pocket to cover the tab as Jackson settled his hat on his head.

"I'll cover you." Jackson rose to his feet.

Tucker slipped out of the booth, then waited for Leanne to do the same. Without waiting to discuss their options, she headed for the back door in a hurry, as if desperate to get far away from the Diamond County Sheriff's deputies.

SEVEN

After skirting the edge of the table, Leanne's hand went to her hip, as if reaching for a gun.

Did she normally carry a weapon? Her heart thudded against her rib cage as she quickly found the rear exit of the restaurant. As she stepped out into the bright sunlight, she wanted to break into a run. To get as far away from the deputies inside the restaurant as possible.

What was it about the dark brown sheriff's deputy uniforms that brought an instant sense of fear and panic? She remembered having the same reaction when the deputies arrived at the ranch last night.

And why had she reached for a nonexistent gun?

"This way." Tucker cupped her elbow in his hand. He glanced around, then nodded to the building across the street. "We may as well head over to the Sun Valley Motel."

"Okay." She peered over her shoulder, half expecting to see the Diamond County sheriff's deputies following them. Thankfully, all she saw was a restaurant employee tossing a bag of garbage in the dumpster.

Willing her pulse to settle down, she picked up the pace. She was anxious to get inside before the deputies left the restaurant.

Had they come this way just to find her? That didn't

make sense, but she couldn't shake off the sense that the pair of deputies didn't have any legitimate business in Austin.

And that they were up to no good. She didn't like thinking they were dirty cops, but the irrational fear wouldn't leave her alone.

If only she could remember!

She reached up and fingered the gold cross at her throat. *Please, Lord Jesus, show me the way. Heal my wounds, especially my missing memory!*

The whispered prayer helped her relax. And when they crossed the street and entered the motel lobby, a sense of relief washed over her.

For some reason, she felt the need to stay hidden from the Diamond County sheriff's deputies.

She stood off to the side, facing the main lobby door, as Tucker arranged for a pair of connecting rooms. She wasn't surprised that he convinced the clerk to let him pay in cash.

They waited for another ten minutes before Jackson arrived in the SUV.

Tucker handed her one of the keys, then gave another one to Jackson. "We're in connecting rooms. Jackson and I are in room seven, and your key will access room eight."

She nodded, and followed the two men down the row of rooms. From what she could tell, many were vacant.

"I'd like you to unlock your side of the connecting door," Tucker said as he opened room seven.

"Okay." She unlocked her door and stepped inside. The room was nothing fancy, but she appreciated the scent of pine-scented cleaner in the air. She quickly crossed over to unlock her side.

"I stopped to chat with them. They were vague about what they were doing out this way," Jackson was saying.

"After an awkward pause, Deputy Gomez said something about checking the status of a prisoner. His partner, Deputy Barnes, quickly agreed."

"Sounds fishy to me." Tucker scowled.

"Oh yeah." Jackson nodded. "The way they were scanning the restaurant customers told me they were looking for someone. But I didn't let my suspicions show. I pretended to accept their story at face value."

"Does that mean you believe me?" She glanced between the two men. "You really think a dirty cop could be a part of this?"

"Yeah, I do." Tucker held her gaze. "For one thing, your reaction was instantaneous. Not to mention, you were right about how they were way outside their jurisdiction."

She wanted to hug him for his support.

"You may want to call our boss," Jackson drawled.

"Yeah. Not only does Owens need an update, but part of our role is to investigate potential dirty cops."

Leanne sank into the closest chair. "What does your boss think about me? You mentioned he wanted to meet face-to-face."

Tucker exchanged a quick look with Jackson before answering. "I think he believes you. I explained about the gunfire and your memory loss. I had to give him a good reason to get the evidence processed so quickly. I didn't mention the disappearing dead body, but maybe I should have, as it may pertain to the possibility of dirty cops being involved." He shrugged. "Either way, it might be good to get the governor's approval to work the case."

"There's something you should know." Both men stared at Leanne expectantly. "When we left the restaurant, my right hand went to my hip as if to reach for a weapon."

"So you are working in law enforcement?"

She held up her hands in frustration. "How should I know, Tucker? It seems odd that I wouldn't be dressed in a uniform if that was the case." Reaching for a gun hadn't been a conscious thought. And it was the first time she'd done that since losing her memory.

Tucker's phone rang. "This is the lab." He quickly lifted the device to his ear. "Hello. Ranger Powell speaking."

She twisted her fingers in her lap, wondering what else she might do by instinct, rather than memory, as Tucker listened to the other end of the call.

"You'all are sure about that?" Another pause. "Okay, thanks."

She knew from the resigned expression on his face that the blood on her clothing matched that found at the site of the dead body.

She really had killed a man.

A wave of anguish hit her hard. She jumped up and bolted over the threshold to her room. Tears pricked her eyes.

She'd killed a man!

Collapsing on the end of her bed, she buried her face in her hands. Why was this hitting her so hard? All along, it seemed obvious that her arriving at the ranch house wearing bloodstained clothes was connected to the dead body found on the same property.

A dead body that was taken away while they were distracted by gunfire.

Who was he? Did the guy have a family? Wife? Kids?

Maybe it was a delayed reaction to everything that had transpired since she'd arrived on Tucker's ranch, but deep sobs erupted from her throat. And once the dam burst, it seemed as if she might never stop crying.

"Leanne, don't torture yourself like this." The mattress

dipped as Tucker sat beside her. He wrapped his arm around her shoulders, drawing her in for a warm hug. "Don't imagine the worst-case scenario. We'll figure out what happened."

He was being so sweet and supportive that she gave in to the desperate need to soak up his strength. Turning, she buried her face into the hollow of his shoulder. He held her close as she struggled to stop crying.

"It's okay. You're fine," he murmured. And she almost smiled as she imagined him saying the same thing to one of his horses.

The image helped, enabling her to draw in one long, deep breath, then another. She managed to pull herself together, sniffling loudly.

"Thank you." Her low husky voice was muffled against his now-damp shirt.

"Anytime."

In no hurry to move, she rested against him for a long moment. Being held by Tucker was a soothing balm to her nerves, the complete opposite reaction from the fear she'd felt at seeing the Diamond County sheriff's deputies.

Finally, she forced herself to push away. Avoiding his gaze, she wiped at her face with her hands. "Sorry about getting you soaked."

"It'll dry." This easygoing side of Tucker was a novelty. He'd been so suspicious of her from the moment she'd crawled through Pops's bedroom window.

Feeling better, she lifted her head to face him. His intense green eyes made her shiver.

Not from fear, but an acute sense of anticipation. Tucker was too ruggedly handsome for his own good.

He didn't say anything but leaned closer with a slow, deliberate movement. She found herself leaning toward him, too. And when his gaze dropped to her mouth, she knew he was going to kiss her.

Tension sizzled between them.

"Hey, Tuck? Boss wants to talk to you." Jackson's voice made Tucker pull back as if he'd been doused with a bucket of ice water.

"Coming." He jumped up, stumbling over his own two feet in his haste to put distance between them. Then he hesitated. "Will you be okay?"

She couldn't possibly be okay until she knew who she was and what had happened, but that wasn't what he meant. She managed a nod, her throat too tight to answer.

He raked his hand through his thick sandy-brown hair in a gesture of frustration, but turned and headed for the connecting doorway. After drawing in a deep fortifying breath, she followed.

She wanted to listen to Tucker's side of the conversation, but as she hovered in the doorway, she couldn't seem to tear her gaze away from his lean, muscular figure.

Why was she suddenly so aware of him? He hadn't even kissed her, but the near miss had sent her pulse skyrocketing.

Ridiculous physical response, considering she didn't know for absolute certainty her name, her career or anything else about herself. There was also the matter of her personal life. She wanted to believe she wasn't involved with anyone, but what if she was? Could she really be attracted to another man?

This sudden awareness of Tucker was a complication she didn't need. She wasn't even sure she liked him, much less trusted him. She wanted to believe she was a cop, too, but if there was any hint she'd committed a crime, he'd be quick to arrest her.

Kissing him was out of the question. End of story.

But when he lowered the phone and caught her gaze, her cheeks heated with the realization that she hadn't heard a single word he'd said.

So much for her attempt to stay focused on the case surrounding her missing memory. She was far too aware of her conflicted feelings for Tucker Powell.

Tucker couldn't believe he'd almost kissed Leanne. A woman he barely knew. A woman who might be a cop, or a criminal. He wanted to kick himself for getting so close to her.

He could blame the situation, but the truth was, he hadn't been able to ignore her tears.

"What's up?" Jackson's comment broke into Tucker's thoughts.

"Boss has given us the go-ahead to work the case." He dragged his gaze from Leanne to Jackson. The glint of amusement in Jackson's eyes spoke volumes. As if his buddy knew full well the dilemma he'd gotten himself into. He cleared his throat. "The blood match between Leanne's clothes and the scene of the dead body clinched the deal."

"I figured he would." Jackson shrugged. "Why not? The case fell right into your lap. And the fact that you were shot at twice more here in Austin means the gunman has crossed jurisdictions."

Since that was verbatim what their boss Captain John Owens had said, he nodded. "Exactly. For starters, we need the laptop." The sooner Tuck could confirm Leanne's identity, the better. "I'd like to search for any and all information we can find on *Leanne Wolfe*."

Jackson nodded. "I'll grab it. Do you want me to head over to get your SUV, too?"

"That would be great, thanks." Tucker couldn't wait to log into the system. Work would be his salvation, the way it had been after Cherry had cheated on him eighteen months ago. It would help keep his head screwed on straight.

Jackson left the room, and returned a moment later with the laptop. Tuck set the laptop on the table and handed over the keys to the car.

After Jackson left to retrieve the SUV, Tucker glanced at Leanne. "You might want to take the opportunity to rest. I know you still have a headache, and sleep may be the best way to get your memory back."

She crossed her arms over her chest and stepped closer to the small table. "I have a vested interest in the case. I'd like to know more about what happened out on the ranch, too."

He swallowed a sigh. He couldn't blame her for needing to know what they uncovered. But he didn't relish having her looming over his shoulder.

A beautiful distraction he didn't need.

"Fine." He gestured to the second chair. "Close your eyes and give me some time to work. I'll let you know when I find something."

She frowned but didn't argue. She dropped into the chair, her knees bumping his.

The motel room suddenly seemed too small and cramped. Ignoring her as best he could, he logged into the work laptop. Rather than going through his email, he opened a browser window to type her name, Leanne Wolfe, into the search bar.

He paused, then turned the screen toward her. "Is that the correct spelling of your first name?"

She nibbled her lower lip, shrugged and nodded. "I think so."

"Let's see what we can find." He turned the screen back so he could see it and hit Enter.

Several articles were displayed on the screen, none having anything to do with a woman who looked like Blondie. There was an author, an actress and others.

Of course it couldn't be that easy. He scrolled through the list. He'd anticipated that if Leanne was involved in something illegal, the information would be at the top of the search engine.

But that hadn't happened.

He hadn't gotten far down the list when Jackson returned, dropping the key fob on the table. "Get this. The Diamond County deputies are still at the restaurant."

"Really?" He leaned back in his chair and glanced at his watch with a frown. "Why would they hang around?"

"Don't know," Jackson admitted. "But I did my best to make sure they didn't see me getting behind the wheel of the SUV. I figured that would only spark more questions."

"I'm sure they're looking for me." Leanne's expression was somber.

He glanced at her. "Maybe. Or they're waiting for someone else to show up." No way did he think the deputies came all the way to Austin to have lunch at the family restaurant. As Leanne had suggested, they'd come this far for a reason.

"I wish I knew what was going on," Leanne said. "Like how the deputies even knew you brought me to Austin."

He thought about the black truck following them, then being shot at by the driver of the silver truck. And one of those two shooters showing up at the apartment building. "The guys driving the pickup trucks knew we were close to Austin." Then another thought occurred to him. "I called the Diamond County deputies last night. I ended up downplaying the whole thing once we knew the dead guy had been removed. But those two cops who responded know I'm a Ranger."

There was a long moment of silence as they considered the various possibilities.

None of them good.

"I don't like this. I'll walk over and sneak in the back door so I can keep an eye on them. Maybe they are waiting to meet with someone. If so, I'll get a few pictures to see if Leanne can recognize anyone."

"Thanks, Jackson." With only one computer between them, there wasn't much that Jackson could do to help search, anyway. "Call me if something interesting happens."

"Will do." Jackson settled his hat back on his head and left.

"I hope they are meeting someone." Leanne frowned. "I hate feeling as if my entire life is hanging in limbo."

More like hanging in the center of a bull's-eye, but he didn't say the words. While he wanted to reassure her, they didn't know much more than they did last night.

The last name *Wolfe* at the apartment building along with the blood match between her clothes and the dead guy were the only leads they had thus far.

That wasn't saying much.

Then again, it wasn't as if their trip had been uneventful. Between the gunfire on the highway and the gunman who'd found them at the apartment, they had narrowly escaped being killed.

Resisting the urge to reach over to squeeze her hand, he focused his attention on the laptop. He started back at the top, to make sure he hadn't missed anything.

Leanne leaned forward, resting her head on her folded

arms. A flash of sympathy caught him off guard. Why was he letting her get under his skin?

No clue.

His phone rang, startling him. Seeing Marsh's name, his gut tensed as he quickly answered. "Hey Marsh, what's wrong?"

"Nothing. Stacy, is here, and Pops is doing well," Marsh said quickly. "It's been quiet, so I thought I'd check in. I heard about Sam and Mari going to the emergency department for treatment. That only leaves Jackson to help you investigate this thing."

"Yeah, but we're doing okay." He glanced at Leanne, who he suspected was listening to his side of the conversation, even though she hadn't lifted her head. "A couple of Diamond County deputies are having lunch at the restaurant across the street from the Sun Valley Motel. Jackson headed over to keep an eye on them. We think they may be meeting with someone."

"That's strange," Marsh said. "As I walked the perimeter about three hours ago, I saw a Diamond County squad car go past the ranch driveway, heading northeast. I didn't think much about it, as the ranch happens to be in their jurisdiction. But they shouldn't be anywhere near Austin."

"Exactly."

"Be careful out there," Marsh warned. "Do you need anything?"

"No, we've got it covered. I'd rather you stay out at the Rocking T." It was only a few hours ago that a dead man had been found, then removed from the property. That, along with the several bouts of gunfire, was enough to concern him. "I can't do this unless I know Pops and Stacy are safe."

"Okay." Marsh didn't seem upset at playing the role of protector. "Call if anything changes."

"I will." He ended the call and set his phone on the table. He scrubbed his hands over his face, willing the exhaustion away.

"I can make coffee." He turned to find Leanne watching him. "You look like you need it."

"Thanks." He tapped the keyboard to bring the computer screen to life. He refreshed the page, intending to try different search terms when a new headline popped up on the screen.

"Border Patrol Agent Leanne J. Wolfe Wanted for the Murder of Troy Gonzales."

Murder? He stared at the screen in shock, realizing the dead man who'd been dragged off the Rocking T Ranch was likely this Troy Gonzales.

His original assumption was right. Leanne had killed him.

EIGHT

Leanne turned from the coffeemaker, frowning at the stricken expression on Tucker's features. She handed him a fresh cup of coffee, even as she mentally braced herself for bad news. "What's wrong?"

He took the cup, set it aside then held her gaze. "Does the name *Troy Gonzales* mean anything to you?"

"Troy Gonzales," she repeated. The name was oddly familiar, but she couldn't conjure a memory of the man. "I'm sorry, but I don't remember him. Although by the look on your face, it seems like I should."

"He may have worked with you."

She shook her head, feeling impatient. "That doesn't help. Just tell me what's going on."

With a grim expression, Tucker tapped the keyboard, then turned the screen so that she could see it. The headline—*Border Patrol Agent Leanne J. Wolfe Wanted for the Murder of Troy Gonzales*—made her knees go weak.

She dropped into the chair, her mind whirling. She'd killed a man.

She had actually killed a man!

Lord, have mercy! Please show me the truth!

Her panicked prayer went unanswered. The headline on the screen mocked her.

"As you can see by the article, you work as a border patrol agent," Tucker went on. "Does that sound familiar?"

Dazed, she nodded, the image of a green uniform flashing in her mind. She remembered how she'd reached for a gun that wasn't there. It seemed right that she worked for the border patrol. Although how on earth she'd gotten into that line of work was a mystery.

"Do you know what shift you work?" His question was casual, and to her surprise the answer popped into her mind.

"Midnights. I work the midnight shift."

His eyebrows levered upright. "That's great. Do you remember anything else?"

Her headache intensified as she tried to remember being at work in her uniform. But the haze in her mind only seemed to get worse, rather than better.

"No." She hated feeling so helpless.

He looked disappointed. "At least this explains why you often sound as if you work in law enforcement."

She nodded, her thoughts whirling. Troy Gonzales was dead. And it seemed obvious to her that it was his body that she and Tucker had found on the ranch. She also remembered how Tucker had all but accused her of stabbing him.

"I didn't kill him." She pushed the words through her tight throat.

He grimaced and shrugged as if he wasn't sure what to believe. He gestured to the computer screen. "I didn't say you did, but you may want to read the article for yourself."

Swallowing hard, she did.

Border Patrol Agent Leanne J. Wolfe is wanted for the murder of her colleague, Agent Troy Gonzales, who died of a stab wound to the abdomen. We ask that anyone with information on the whereabouts of

Leanne J. Wolfe to call the Diamond County Sheriff's Department as soon as possible.

"The Diamond County Sheriff's Department," she repeated, then frowned, glancing at Tucker. "Why would they have jurisdiction? If Troy Gonzales is a border patrol agent, wouldn't the Department of Homeland Security be involved? At the very least, they would turf the investigation to the feds."

Tucker arched a brow. "That's true. Even the Rangers wouldn't have jurisdiction over something like that. We work for the governor. However, if Gonzales's body was found in Diamond County and they have reason to believe you killed him, they may be operating under the assumption that this is a personal matter. One that was strictly between the two of you, not involving a threat to homeland security."

Realization dawned. "You mean like a lovers' spat. Or a general physical or sexual assault case that got out of hand."

He nodded. "Exactly."

She couldn't tear her gaze from the screen, wanting desperately to believe she hadn't killed anyone. That if she had stabbed Troy in the abdomen, it had been an act of self-defense.

Not murder.

Troy's blood had been on her clothes and hands. She scrubbed her hands against the fabric of Stacy's borrowed jeans, as if to remove the invisible stain.

"I didn't kill him," she repeated. Her voice reeked of desperation.

Tucker sighed. "Oddly enough, I believe you. For one thing, we know the body was moved from the Rocking T Ranch. Second, we've been targeted by gunmen nonstop. The fact that the Diamond County Sheriff's Department has issued your arrest warrant smells of a setup. Obviously, they want to pin Gonzales's murder on you, and they'll come up with some story as to how and why that happened." He paused. "To be honest, it also makes things more complicated."

She understood his dilemma. "As a law enforcement officer, you're now aiding and abetting a criminal. And you're worried your boss will order you to bring me in."

"Yes." He raked a hand through his sandy hair. "I can hold Captain Owens off for a while, especially since we have our suspicions about the Diamond County deputies, but we need proof. Evidence of some sort to back up your story." He sighed. "It would really help if your memory would return."

As if she didn't want that more than anything, too? She almost snapped back at him, but managed to bite her tongue. The situation wasn't his fault.

It was hers. For dragging him into this. For showing up on up on his grandfather's ranch covered in Troy's blood with a gunman on her tail.

And no memory of how she'd gotten there.

Tucker may have viewed her with suspicion, but he'd also been gracious and supportive. Putting his life on the line to protect her.

"Okay." She forced herself to think logically. "If the bad guys want to set me up as Troy's murderer, then why fire shots at us?"

He shrugged. "That's bothering me, too."

"Tracking me on the ranch makes sense. They could have claimed I was a fugitive fleeing the scene of the crime. Killing me then and there would have put an end to it, tying the loose ends in a pretty bow." A chill snaked down her spine at how close she'd come to being killed last night.

"Yep. I can see how they'd play that angle," Tucker said. "If I didn't know any better, I'd have believed them."

She couldn't blame him for that. If the situation was reversed, she was sure she'd have believed it, too.

But deep down, she knew she didn't break the law. She stared at him. "Thanks to you rescuing me, that didn't happen. But rather than letting me go and simply issuing an arrest warrant, they took a shot at you the following morning." The image of his cowboy hat with a bullet hole in the crown was all too clear in her mind. "Then they took it a step further, following us to Austin and taking shots at us on the highway. Finally, they had someone stationed outside the apartment building in a last attempt to kill me." She frowned and spread her hands. "How in the world did they plan to explain away all of that?"

"That's a good point," he admitted. "Keep in mind, they're not aware of your memory loss. At least, I don't know how they could know about it, since we never went to a hospital. Or talked about it in public. But that aside, there must be a significant criminal element to this. Something they can use against you once they have you in custody."

The thought made her sick. And it suddenly occurred to her that the reason her mind had shut down so drastically was because she hadn't wanted to remember killing Troy. Especially if she knew him on a personal level.

She closed her eyes, willing the thought away. Going down that path wasn't helpful. She lightly touched the cross around her neck.

While she didn't remember anything useful, she knew she was a woman of faith. All she could do now was lean on prayer and hope that God allowed her memory to return.

Before anyone else got hurt.

* * *

The angst etched in Leanne's features was too real to be faked. Time for him to put his earlier suspicions aside and to come at this investigation from the premise that she was being framed for murder.

Now, he just needed to figure out how to convince Captain Owens of that fact. The multiple shooting attempts did work in their favor.

His phone rang, startling him. He quickly answered Jackson's call. "What's up?"

"The deputies and the man they had lunch with are leaving now," Jackson whispered. "I was too far away to hear what they discussed. The new guy wasn't wearing a uniform, but that doesn't mean he's not on a law enforcement payroll. I'd like to follow the new guy. Maybe he'll head someplace interesting."

"Go. But be careful."

"Will do." Jackson ended the call.

"Who was that?" Leanne asked.

"Jackson. He apparently watched our deputies meet with a guy in street clothes. They're leaving the restaurant, so he's following the newbie."

Her blue eyes lit up with hope. "Do you think the new guy is one of the gunmen?"

That possibility had crossed his mind, and he quickly texted Jackson. *Send photos if you have them.*

He waited a beat, but there was no reply. Likely, Jackson was already on the road tailing the mystery man. Tucker set his phone on the table, knowing Jackson was smart enough to have taken pictures of the meetup as evidence, and would likely send them along when he had a chance.

It wasn't easy to sit here at the motel twiddling his thumbs, while Jackson did the legwork on the case. Yet as much as Tucker wished he could be more actively involved, the truth was that he was a target now, too.

Whoever was trying to kill Leanne must believe she'd told him what she knew. Remembering how the man driving the silver truck had turned to look at him seconds before firing his gun proved it.

But that didn't mean he was helpless. He reached for the now-lukewarm coffee and took a long sip before turning the computer back toward him.

He brought up a search engine and typed in *Troy Gonzales* and *border patrol*. An instant later, the guy's image bloomed on the screen.

Looking at the professional photo of Gonzales dressed in his green uniform, it was clear he was the man with the stab wound. Once again, he turned the screen so Leanne could see the picture.

"Does this help spark any memories?"

Her expression turned somber as she looked at the photograph of the man who was likely her colleague. "No. But I must work with him, right?" She rubbed her temples. "It seems wrong not to remember him."

"How are you feeling? Maybe you should try to get some sleep. I can't help but think that resting your mind is the best way to recover your memory."

"Maybe." She looked so dejected that his heart ached for her. Reading the article about how she was wanted for murder couldn't have been easy.

"Leanne." He reached over to take her hand. He ignored the tingle of awareness that rippled over his skin. For all he knew, she had been dating Troy. If not him, then someone else. "We're safe here."

"I know." She clung to his hand for a moment. "I owe you my life, Tucker."

He released her hand, not wanting her gratitude. "You don't owe me anything. Anyone would have done the same thing."

She shook her head sadly. "Not without turning me in." She glanced at the computer, then back at him. "I think we need to go back to my apartment building."

He frowned. "It's not like we have a key."

She waved a hand. "We can break in. The point is that if I live there, I may have left evidence behind." Her eyes brightened with hope. "Maybe seeing where I live, my clothes and other personal items, will help spur my memory."

Again, she had a point. "I don't know," he said slowly.

"We have to try." She frowned. "Although, it strikes me as odd that I live in Austin if I'm a border patrol agent. The cost of living is higher, and it's not exactly close to any of the checkpoints. Talk about inconvenient."

"Maybe you live with someone." A man? Maybe even Troy Gonzales? The idea of finding a photograph or other evidence of Leanne being in a relationship made him feel like a jerk for almost kissing her.

"I would never live with a man, even platonically. I'd have to be sharing the place with another woman. And I can't imagine that there are many female border patrol agents." She shrugged. "In most law enforcement agencies, women are in the minority."

Her Christian values shone through, despite her inability to remember her past. And he was struck again by how much her faith was a part of her. So much so that she instinctively prayed without knowing her own name.

Humbling to have that level of faith. He wondered if there was something to be said for leaning on God during troubled times. And thanking Him for their blessings.

"All the more reason we should head over there to examine the apartment," Leanne said, interrupting his thoughts.

"Okay, we'll check the place out. But not until dark. We need to let enough time go by to ensure the crime scene has been vacated."

She looked as if she wanted to argue, but then nodded. "Okay, you're right. Besides, we need to make sure Jackson is back, too."

"Great." In all honesty, it felt good to have a plan of action. Especially since breaking into her apartment might give them something concrete to go on. Clues or fragments of memories. He would take either one. "Meanwhile, you should rest. I'll see if I can find anything useful on Troy Gonzales."

"I'd rather help you."

He swallowed a groan. The last thing he wanted was Leanne hovering over his shoulder. He was far too aware of her nearness already.

Maybe Gonzales was happily married? He almost laughed out loud at his wishful thinking.

Doing his best to ignore Leanne, he continued his search. Unfortunately, other than finding Troy Gonzales's professional photograph, and the article naming Leanne as his murder suspect, Tucker didn't find anything helpful.

He tried social media next but, again, came up empty. Which made sense, as most law enforcement officials didn't plaster their personal lives all over the internet.

It was too early for an obituary, but he made a mental note to check back on that possibility later. Surely Gonzales had someone close to him who would step up to plan his funeral.

Leanne stood and stretched. "I think I will take a nap. Watching you work is making my headache worse."

"I think that's a good idea." He hoped his relief wasn't too obvious. "You need to take care of yourself."

"I will." She moved toward the threshold of their connecting rooms, then paused to glance back at him. "You'll wake me if you learn anything important?"

"Yes." He offered a reassuring smile. "I'm sure Jackson will fill us in soon."

She nodded, then disappeared into the adjoining room. He let out a soundless sigh and turned back to the computer screen.

There had to be a way to find more information on Troy Gonzales. Or Leanne? Energized, he typed her name and job title into the search engine.

As with Troy, her professional photograph bloomed on the screen. Like all cop photos, her expression was serious, her blond hair pulled back from her face and secured in a bun.

She was still beautiful, but she also came across as a capable law enforcement professional. Her background—and Troy's, too, for that matter—would be checked in depth before being granted a job working for the Department of Homeland Security.

He wondered what had drawn her to the profession, then continued his search. Twenty minutes later, he gave up, having learned nothing helpful.

Without Leanne's memory, they were at a distinct disadvantage. They had no idea who was responsible for killing Gonzales or why.

And it was only a matter of time before Owens would call with a request to bring her in.

Yet, he couldn't help but think that arresting Leanne was playing into the killers' hands. That once she was in custody, she would end up dead. Especially since he knew the Diamond County Sheriff's Department was involved.

And they'd already proven they were willing to kill to hide the truth.

He stared at his phone, willing Jackson to call. His buddy hadn't been gone long, but he was anxious to hear what, if anything, he'd found.

As if on cue, his phone vibrated with an incoming text message. Grabbing the phone, he pressed the button to open the messages.

It took a moment, since the motel internet was slow, but soon several pictures bloomed on the screen. Heart racing, he clicked on the first one, then used his thumbs to zoom in on the image. This could be just what they needed to prove Leanne's innocence!

There was one man seated at the table with the two deputies. This view only displayed his profile, which didn't look familiar.

Tucker moved onto the next image, which wasn't nearly as clear as the first. He tried not to groan out loud. Jackson had taken the photos from a distance, and while he must have zoomed in, they weren't great.

The third picture was the best. After enlarging the photograph, he stared intently at the man's face, trying to mesh this image with the brief memory of the driver of the silver truck who'd shot at them as he'd passed on the right.

After a long moment, he was forced to admit they were not the same man. This guy in the picture, whoever he was, hadn't been the driver of the silver truck. He might have been the one following in the black truck, but there was no way to know for sure.

Tucker hated to admit the photographs of the meeting Jackson had witnessed were nothing but a dead end.

They were no closer to having the evidence they needed to prove Leanne hadn't murdered anyone. And time was not on their side. If they didn't find something soon, Owens might decide to toss Leanne in jail and pull them off the case.

NINE

Leanne peered through the window overlooking the parking lot outside the motel, then tugged the curtains closed to block the bright sunlight. She crawled into bed and pulled the blanket up to her chin.

For long moments, she stared blindly at the ceiling. She was too keyed up to relax. And despite Tucker's suggestion, she was certain that falling asleep would be impossible. The headline for the article Tucker had found reverberated in her mind.

Border Patrol Agent Leanne J. Wolfe Wanted for the Murder of Troy Gonzales.

Murder!

Jean. She abruptly sat up, her heart pounding. Her middle name was Jean. Leanne Jean Wolfe.

She was named after her mother, Jean.

Hope bloomed in her heart. Was this a sign of her memory returning? *Please, Lord Jesus, help me remember!*

But no other tidbits of her past came to the forefront of her mind. She blew out a breath and lay back down, resting her head on the pillow. As much as she was glad to know her middle name was Jean, she would rather remember what had transpired when Troy Gonzales was murdered.

Especially if she was the one who'd stabbed him.

Closing her eyes, she took several slow, deep breaths. *Breathe in, hold for four seconds, then breathe out and hold for four seconds.* She focused on relaxing every muscle in her body. Yet even with the drapes closed, there was still too much light shining in.

But that wasn't unusual, was it? Not if she worked the midnight shift.

She tried to clear her mind. To open her heart to prayer. Last night, she'd been so exhausted, mentally and physically, that she hadn't had trouble falling asleep. Especially with her pounding headache.

But this was different. There was too much information flashing in her mind.

Most of it distressing.

After what seemed like forever, she finally relaxed to the point of drifting off.

You think you're so smart? You'll never tell anyone what you know.

Let her go.

Not a chance.

No, Troy! Don't!

Troy leaped in front of her, just as the knife plunged deep. She screamed, clutching him as he sagged against her.

Noooo!

Leanne awoke with a start, sweat beading her brow. She pressed a hand to her racing heart. The dream had been so real. As if it had really happened. But was that possible? Had she only dreamed the scenario? Or was it an actual memory?

Had Troy really jumped in front of her when he'd been stabbed? Had he taken the blade meant for her?

"Leanne?" Tucker poked his head through the connecting door. "Are you okay? I heard you cry out."

"I don't know." She wiped the sweat from her brow, and swung her legs over so she was sitting at the edge of the bed. Her hair was stuck to the side of her face, and she brushed it back impatiently. "I had a dream. Or a memory. I'm not sure which."

"Really?" His green eyes brightened with interest. He stepped closer and rested a reassuring hand on her shoulder. "Tell me."

She swallowed hard. "I was with Troy. We were outside, in the evening, the sun was just sliding down over the horizon. There was another man there, too, but I can't picture him. He was saying something about me not being smart and that I'd never tell anyone what I knew. Then he thrust a knife toward me, but Troy jumped in front of me in the nick of time. The blade sank deep into his stomach, and I screamed." She shivered, despite the warmth of the room, and raised her gaze to his. "That's all. It seemed to go on forever, but now that I'm telling you, the timeframe was probably a minute, maybe less."

Tucker nodded. "That's how dreams are sometimes. But now that you're awake, what does your gut tell you? Is that what really happened?"

She shook her head, feeling helpless. "How can I know that for sure? I can't even tell you what the other man looked like! The entire thing may have been just a dream." She shivered again. "Or a nightmare. Maybe that's an alternate scenario my brain came up with to make me feel better. Because I don't want to believe I killed Troy."

His hand tightened on her shoulder. "I think your mind is starting to heal. That you're slowly but surely beginning to remember what happened."

She desperately wanted to believe that. "I remembered my middle name is Jean. Leanne Jean Wolfe."

His eyebrows shot up. "See? That proves my point."

She nodded, then rose to her feet. "I need a few minutes."

"Take your time." He stepped back, giving her room. She sought refuge in the bathroom. After splashing cold water on her face, she stared at her reflection in the mirror.

She'd hoped remembering would bring a level of peace, but the result was just the opposite. The brief memory, if that's what that was, only opened more questions without answers.

Had Troy saved her life? What had she found that had caused a man to try to stab her?

And who was the man responsible? Why couldn't she see his face? Why?

I will fear no evil: for thou art with me (Psalm 23:4).

The Bible verse flashed in her mind. She couldn't remember where she'd heard it before, but the words brought a sense of peace.

There was no reason to be afraid. God was with her. And she knew with His help, she would remember everything.

Hopefully sooner rather than later.

After drying her face on the towel, she left the bathroom. Tucker had gone back into his room, and she could hear him on the phone.

"Yes, sir. I understand. If you could get the images run through the facial recognition program, I'm sure we'll know more."

Her gut tightened. The solemn respect in Tucker's voice made her think he was talking to his boss, Captain John Owens.

"Thanks again." Tucker lowered the phone and glanced at her. "Better?"

"Yes." She forced a smile she didn't feel. "Was that your boss?"

He nodded. "Don't worry, he hasn't given the order for you to be taken into custody."

Not yet. But she decided to think positively. The more time she was given to remember, the better. "That's good. What was that about facial recognition?"

"Oh yeah. I almost forgot. Just a minute." He worked the phone screen, and it looked to her as if he was sending a message off to his boss. Then he nodded. "Take a look at these pictures." He thumbed the screen then handed the device to her. "Do any of them look familiar?"

She stared down at the photos. A man in street clothes sat between the two Diamond County deputies. She moved from that picture to the next. And finally the last one, which offered the best view of the suspect. She was disappointed not to experience a flash of recognition. "No, I can't say that he looks like anyone I know." She lifted her gaze to his. "Could he be one of the shooters?"

"Maybe. Do you remember him from the shooting on the highway?"

"I had my head down, so I didn't get a good look at him." She flushed. "To be honest, the gun pointed at you was a bit of a distraction."

"Yeah, for me, too. But I'm pretty sure the driver of the silver truck is not this guy who met with the deputies." He shrugged and took the phone back. "He could have been the driver in the black truck. Or the guy posted outside your apartment. Since he met with the deputies here, I'd say for sure he was the shooter at your apartment."

She sighed. Apparently, these guys were smart enough to keep the shooter Tucker had seen out of the picture.

Leaving them with nothing more to go on than their suspicions. And the gaping holes in her memory.

* * *

Tucker was a little worried that Jackson had been gone for so long, although he did his best not to show it. He glanced at the alarm clock near the bed. "Are you hungry?"

Leanne shrugged. "I could eat, but I would rather not head over to the restaurant across the street. We would be better off stopping at a fast-food restaurant on the way back to my apartment."

"Not yet." He glanced at the window. Autumn meant dusk fell earlier now, but he wasn't going anywhere until he heard from Jackson. "It's not dark enough."

They stood awkwardly for a moment, before Tucker turned back to the computer. When his phone rang, he nearly dropped it in his haste to answer. "Jackson! Where are you?"

"I lost him," Jackson said with disgust. "I hate to say it, but he must have made me. I backtracked, trying to figure out where he went, but gave up. The only thing I can say for sure is that he was headed south, toward the Mexico border."

Tucker masked his disappointment. "Hey, that's something. And I'm sure he was in Diamond County when you lost him, right?"

"Probably," Jackson admitted.

"Thanks for the pictures. I sent them to Owens to have them run through facial rec. Hopefully, we'll get a name on him very soon."

"That would help." Jackson sounded frustrated. "I'll be there shortly."

Before Tucker could say anything more, his buddy ended the call.

"He lost him in Diamond County?" Leanne had obviously listened to his side of the call. "That's a bummer. I wish we had more to go on."

He did, too. "We'll get his name soon enough."

"We really need to get into my apartment." Her blue eyes gleamed with anticipation. "Too bad I live on the third floor, or we could have simply broken a window. As it stands, you'll be forced to kick the door in to get inside."

He grimaced. "Believe it or not, I can pick locks. I even have a couple of tools in my wallet. But we'll have to be quick so that we don't attract undue attention from your neighbors. And we'll need to wait for someone to leave to even enter the building."

"I know, but with six floors of apartments, I'm sure someone is always coming or going." She didn't appear concerned.

He caught a glimpse of movement out the window and quickly rose for a closer look. Jackson was pulling an extra-large pizza box from the back seat of the SUV.

Great minds. Tuck opened the door for Jackson.

"I brought dinner, because I'm hungry and you're slacking on keeping us fed," Jackson said as he entered the room. He glanced at Leanne. "I probably should have called to ask before getting this. I hope you like your pizza with the works."

"That's fine with me." She moved the laptop out of the way to make room.

Tucker's mouth watered as Jackson lifted the lid of the box. "Smells great."

"Oh yeah." Jackson grinned. "I needed something to cheer me up."

Tucker chuckled. "Food always helps."

"I agree. Although I would like to say grace." Leanne bowed her head and waited a beat. "Dear Lord Jesus, we ask You to bless this food we are about to eat. We ask that You continue to guide us on Your path as we seek the truth. Amen."

"Amen," he and Jackson echoed.

Praying before meals was common with Sam and Mari, but somehow this felt different.

More personal. Maybe because Tuck suddenly understood how much he needed God's help to keep Leanne safe.

"Ladies first." He gestured to Leanne.

She helped herself, then Jackson did, too. Jackson sat on the edge of the bed, leaving him the chair next to Leanne. The room felt unusually crowded, but Tucker did his best to ignore the way Leanne's knees bumped his. Jackson sent him an amused glance, as if his growing feelings for Leanne were obvious.

A woman without a memory who was wanted for murder.

They ate in silence for a few minutes. Then Jackson broke the silence, "What's the plan? Other than waiting for an ID on our guy who managed to shake me loose."

Tuck glanced at Leanne. "Leanne wants to head to her apartment to see if she left something behind. Or to see if being there sparks her memories."

Jackson lifted a brow. "That could work, especially in jogging Leanne's memory."

"I'll pick the lock, hopefully without attracting attention."

"On a dead bolt?" Jackson frowned at Tuck. "That's not easy."

"It's not, but I practiced a bit while Leanne rested." He didn't want to sound boastful, but he hadn't done too badly. "I think I can do it."

"You practiced?" Leanne looked impressed. "That was smart."

When they'd finished eating, he stood and set the empty pizza box aside. "We should head out." It was almost seven thirty, and it would take a solid twenty ride into downtown Austin.

Leanne jumped up as if she couldn't wait to get out of there. "I'm ready."

"Hang on. I think we should take the laptop, just in case." Tuck placed it under his arm.

Jackson went for the driver's side, leaving him the passenger's seat. Leanne climbed into the back without complaint. He pushed the laptop under his seat. "I hope that guy you followed didn't get your plate number," he said as Jackson hit the highway.

"I don't think so. Once we were outside of San Antonio, there wasn't much traffic, so I stayed back. A little too far back, as it turned out." Jackson grimaced. "Unless he had someone hiding in the car during their entire lunch meeting, with binoculars, we're good."

Tucker nodded, satisfied. Up ahead, he could see the glow of light from the capitol building. Austin was second to Nashville as being famous for live music, and he decided this was probably the best time to get into the apartment. The hour was late enough that commuters were home from their day jobs, yet early enough that the partygoers weren't out hitting the live-music scene.

They'd need to keep this mission to a sixty-minute round trip or less.

As they approached the apartment building, he leaned forward in his seat. "Drive past, Jackson. Let's make sure there aren't cops lingering nearby." They'd taken the case from the locals, but that didn't mean they wouldn't be hanging around. Watching and waiting for the shooter to return.

"Got it," Jackson said, cruising past.

"Park a few blocks down," Leanne suggested. "We'll approach on foot."

Tuck turned in his seat. "Jackson, I'd like you to stay outside to keep an eye on things. Alert us if you see any cops or something suspicious."

Jackson nodded. "I can do that."

Jackson parked and they all slid from the SUV. By tacit agreement, they split up.

Tuck and Leanne hung around the front of the building for a solid five minutes before some guy came outside. Leanne smiled and grabbed the door, but the guy didn't seem to recognize her. Tuck wasn't sure if that was good or bad.

The way Leanne took the steps to the third floor without breathing hard made him realize she did this on a regular basis. The hallway leading to her apartment was empty, so he quickly went to work on the lock.

Leanne stood in front of him, casting quick and interested glances over her shoulder. His early practice sessions paid off. He was able to gain access without difficulty.

"Stay behind me," he whispered as he pushed the door open. He pulled out his service weapon and panned the room before stepping inside.

There was enough ambient light from outside that he could see fairly well. He quickly cleared the apartment, noticing there was only one bedroom. In the main living space, he opened the small closet, which only had a few women's clothes.

"Can I turn on the light?"

He hesitated, then nodded. Anything to help Leanne remember. "Go ahead."

She turned the switch on a small table lamp, casting a warm glow over the room. She glanced around curiously, then crossed into the small bedroom.

A moment later, she returned. "I wish I could say I remembered living here, but I don't. I can say that I live here alone."

He shouldn't have been relieved at that. "Keep looking. Maybe something will spark a memory."

She scowled, but then made a beeline across the living room. She lifted a picture frame, staring down at the photograph intently.

"What is it?" He braced himself for seeing Leanne with another man. Troy Gonzales? He didn't realize he was holding his breath until he was able to see the picture more clearly.

Leanne was in the photograph, along with another man. An older man, not Gonzales, but someone who shared her facial features and the same blue eyes.

"My dad," she whispered, lightly touching his face with her fingertip. "Frank Wolfe."

His pulse quickened. "You remember him?"

She nodded, her gaze still focused on the photo. "I remember him telling me how proud he was of me." She suddenly frowned, glancing at him. "My mom isn't in the picture. I think she may have passed away."

"We can do a search to find out. Do you remember anything else?"

She slowly shook her head. "No. Just my dad telling me how proud he was of me. We look so happy in this picture."

He smiled, glad she was able to experience a positive memory of her parents.

"I'm bringing this with me." She held the picture frame to her chest. He wasn't sure that was wise, especially if they had to leave the motel in a hurry, but sensed there was no point in arguing.

"Let's go." She abruptly stepped around him.

A sharp crack of gunfire rang out, shattering the living room window. His phone vibrated in his pocket, likely Jackson warning him of the shooter as he tackled Leanne, pinning her to the sofa.

A flash of guilt hit hard. The shooter must have been waiting for them to show up. He never should have brought her back here. Or turned the light on, announcing their presence to anyone who cared to look.

His serious lapse in judgment had almost gotten Leanne killed.

TEN

With her face smashed against the sofa cushions, Leanne struggled to breathe. She squirmed against the weight of Tucker's body. After a moment, he quickly moved to the side, giving her space.

"Stay down," he whispered, lifting his head enough to reach for the lamp. A moment later the room was plunged into darkness.

"I'm sorry." She battled guilt. "I shouldn't have insisted we come here."

"I take full responsibility," Tucker said grimly. "Time to go. You head for the door. I'll cover you from behind."

She nodded, grabbing the picture frame she'd dropped when he'd tackled her. The trip to her apartment didn't help as much as she'd hoped. Other than finding the photo of her father, she hadn't learned anything new.

She'd put Tucker's and Jackson's lives at risk for nothing.

Maintaining a low crouch to avoid being a target, she crossed the room. After a brief pause, she opened the door a crack to peek out, half expecting a second shooter to be there waiting for them.

The hallway was blessedly empty. She was about to turn to let Tucker know when she felt him come up behind her.

"Do you remember if there's a back exit? We can't go toward the front where the shooter is located."

"There is, yes. Right around the corner." She wasn't sure how she knew that, but she didn't hesitate to slip through the door. Rising to her full height, she took the three steps needed to reach the fire exit.

She heard Tucker close her apartment door. They clattered down the concrete stairs, making quick work of the three flights.

"That's okay, just meet us at the SUV."

She didn't have to look over her shoulder to know he was on the phone with Jackson. Tucker's comment indicated Jackson had either lost the gunman or never knew where he was in the first place. She wished more than anything that they could get a line on who this guy was.

"Maybe we should spread out to look for him," she said when they reached ground level.

"Not happening. We need to be far away from here before the cops arrive." His gaze bored into hers. "There's a warrant out for your arrest, remember?"

She winced, having forgotten that tiny problem. Considering how often she'd been targeted by gunfire, it seemed ridiculous to be viewed as a criminal.

But this wasn't the time to argue. She pushed the door open just enough to look outside. The immediate area behind the building was empty, but she could see lights flicking on in several apartments, along with people hovering near windows, checking out the source of the gunfire.

"Run," Tucker whispered. "I'll be right behind you."

Still clutching the picture frame in the crook of her arm, she broke into a jog, hoping the two of them running from the building didn't garner undue attention. Or if it did, that the nosy neighbors were far enough away that they couldn't see them clearly.

She settled into an easy rhythm down one block then the next, ignoring the throbbing pain reverberating in her skull. Somehow, she didn't think running was part of the treatment plan for a head injury.

"Slow down," Tucker said from behind her. "The SUV is up ahead."

She nodded and dropped to a walk. Strangely, she wasn't as short of breath as she'd expected. She'd liked running, even though it made her head hurt. Did she run on a regular basis?

Now that she thought about it, there had been some running gear in the closet. At the time she was more concerned with making sure she lived alone. The near kiss with Tucker had nagged at her, and she'd wanted to be sure she didn't have someone special in her life.

They hovered near the SUV, waiting for Jackson, who had the key fob. He arrived a minute later, clicking the button to unlock the doors.

She quickly slid into the back seat, setting the treasured picture frame next to her. Police sirens filled the air.

They'd gotten away just in time.

"I saw a black truck that I believe belongs to the shooter," Jackson said as he started the engine and pulled away from the curb. He executed a three-point turn to head in the opposite direction of the approaching police cruisers. "I scouted the area, and noted it, but didn't see anyone inside." He grimaced. "You know how many Texans drive trucks. I did jot down the plate number though, just in case. I can't say for sure it's the one the shooter was using, as I was hunkered down between two vehicles when the gunfire rang out. By the time I went back to where I'd seen the truck, it was gone."

"A plate number? That's a start." Tucker sounded relieved. "You did good, Jackson. This isn't your fault. We shouldn't have turned the lamp on. And we should have spent more time scouting the perimeter before going inside." He glanced back at Leanne, his expression grim. "I'm just glad you're not hurt."

"I'm relieved you and Jackson escaped unscathed, too. This was my idea, Tucker. I'm the one who pushed the issue. I can accept responsibility for my mistakes." She sighed. "Seems I'm making several these days."

There was a brief pause before Jackson asked, "I take it you haven't remembered anything that might help?"

Her gaze landed on the picture of her with her father. "No. All we figured out is that I live alone, and I was close to my father. I remembered my dad's name is Frank, but that's about it."

Another long silence hung in the air.

"The trip wasn't a total waste of time if you got a license plate number," Tucker finally said. "We need to get that run through the system ASAP."

"Here." Jackson handed Tucker his phone. "I took a picture of it."

She listened as Tucker called the local police to request a license plate run. She was surprised the dispatcher cooperated so easily, considering the need to send officers to investigate the sound of gunfire.

"We have a name. Dominic Clark." Tucker lowered the phone. "No active warrants for his arrest, and she's sending me his driver's license photo."

She turned the name *Dominic Clark* over in her mind, but it didn't bring forth any memories. As Jackson drove, it occurred to her that it wouldn't take long for the Austin PD to connect the shooting at the apartment to her. After all, her name must be on the lease. Once the cops made that connection, the search for her whereabouts would take center stage.

Although, she figured every cop was on high alert for her already.

"I think we should go to a different motel after this." She caught Jackson's surprised look in the rearview mirror.

Tucker turned in his seat to face her. "Do you think the Sun Valley Motel is compromised?"

"I don't know." It wasn't easy to put her feelings into words. "The restaurant meeting with the deputies may have been a coincidence, but now that a bullet has gone through my apartment window, the cops will be searching for me in earnest. Starting over someplace new seems the smart choice."

"Okay," Tucker agreed. "Good thing I brought the laptop along. Makes it easy to pick a new location."

"We can use the Red Rock Motel," Jackson suggested. "It's located southwest of Austin. Or we could choose San Antonio, to be closer to the ranch and Diamond County."

"Let's stick with Austin for now." Tucker looked relieved. "I'm anxious to dig into this Dominic Clark."

"He may not be involved," Jackson warned. "Let's not jump to conclusions."

Tucker shrugged, and Leanne could tell he'd already decided Dominic was the shooter. "Here's the information now." He played with his phone screen, then frowned. "He's not the same guy you followed from the restaurant."

"I doubted it would be." Jackson shrugged. "That guy was far from Austin when I lost him. I'm not sure there was enough time for him to have backtracked to the apartment to watch the place."

"True. Seems like there are far too many bad guys in this thing. His address is listed as San Antonio, but those are not always up-to-date the way they should be." Tucker turned in his seat to hand her the phone. "Does he look familiar?"

She stared at the driver's license photo of Dominic Clark. Much like when she saw the picture of Troy Gonzales, there was a vague sense of familiarity. Where had she seen this man before?

The memory was there, just out of reach.

"I'm sorry." She passed the phone back to Tucker, feeling more useless than ever.

Dominic Clark may have fired at her and Tucker. She pressed her fingertips to her temples. Somehow, she needed to remember everything. Before anyone else was hurt.

Or worse, killed.

As much as Tucker was filled with regret for placing Leanne in danger, having the identity of a possible perp filled him with hope and anticipation. There were too many coincidences with the shooter and while it was thin, he felt certain they were on the right track.

All he needed was to find a connection between Clark and the Diamond County deputies. From there, they could make the case that Leanne was being framed for Troy Gonzales's murder.

Jackson made good time getting to the Red Rock Motel, a two-story building with at least thirty rooms. He gladly waited with Leanne while Jackson went in to make the arrangements. September wasn't the high tourist season, so he didn't anticipate a problem. And usually their badge assisted in the ability to pay in cash, to avoid leaving a paper trail.

Jackson returned a few minutes later, holding two key cards up for them to see. He slid behind the wheel. "We're on the first floor with connecting rooms fourteen and fifteen. They're at the end of the row."

"Great. Any trouble using cash?" Tucker took the key.

"Nope." Jackson drove past the rooms to park around the back of the building. "We're set."

Tucker pulled the laptop from beneath the seat as Jackson handed Leanne one of the keys.

It didn't take long for the three of them to crowd around the laptop in room fourteen. "I hope we find something on this guy." Leanne sighed.

He did, too. He entered the name *Dominic Clark* with the San Antonio address in the search engine.

Nothing came up.

With a sense of dread, he tried again without the address. Still nothing.

"I told you, this guy may have nothing to do with the shooting," Jackson pointed out. "Or maybe the truck was stolen. Could be Dominic Clark is out of town and doesn't realize someone has taken his truck."

Tucker sat back in his seat, trying to come at this from another angle. On a whim, he typed in *Diamond County Deputy Dominic Clark*.

That worked. The article that bloomed on the screen mentioned Diamond County Deputy Dominic Clark having been injured in the line of duty. The incident happened well over a year ago, but the picture on the screen was a match to the driver's license photo.

He decided to check the Diamond County website to see

if they had photos of their deputies there. But they didn't. There were several job openings posted, but that was all.

Not helpful.

"This is our shooter." He tapped the screen. "I'm sure of it. And it's the link we need between the guys coming after Leanne and the Diamond County Sheriff's Department."

"I don't know about that. The connection is a bit nebulous," Jackson pointed out. "Dominic could claim he loaned his truck to a friend who took it to Austin. I think it's more interesting his address is San Antonio, which isn't in Diamond County."

He shrugged. "There isn't a rule that says you have to live in the county where you work. Diamond County is rather rural and probably doesn't offer much in the way of housing. Then again, the cost of living would be cheaper in those smaller towns along the way, compared to the larger city."

"Diamond County is very close to the border. That's likely how our paths crossed."

Tucker turned to look at Leanne. "I thought you didn't remember him."

"I don't. But if he is our shooter, I must have met him at some point." She frowned, her gaze locked on the screen. "There is something familiar about him. It's frustrating not to know when and where I've seen him before."

The word he would use was *disheartening*. He was growing concerned that Leanne's memory may not return anytime soon. Her apartment, and even seeing the photograph of her father, hadn't worked.

What would help her remember? He didn't know, but he had been counting on her ability to identify the bad guys once she saw them.

His phone rang. Seeing Marsh's name on the screen, his

heart sank as he quickly answered. "Hey Marsh, is everything okay at the ranch?"

"Yeah, everyone is fine," Marsh hastened to reassure him. "But I thought you'd want to know that a couple of deputies were just here looking for you."

"For me?" He caught Leanne's gaze. "Did they say what they wanted?"

"They were following up on your report of finding blood on the property," Marsh said. "I told him that we found an injured cow and assumed the animal was the source of the blood."

He was impressed with Marsh's quick thinking. "What did they say?"

"They seemed surprised by the answer, then asked if we saw anything suspicious over the past twenty-four to forty-eight hours," Marsh went on. "I played dumb, and eventually they admitted that they were here looking for a murder suspect by the name of Leanne Wolfe."

The news shouldn't have surprised him. Obviously, he'd made that initial call about finding blood in the woods, before he knew the body had been taken away and that Leanne was being framed for murder.

"I feel bad that you were put in a position that you had to lie for us," Tucker said. "And I'm sure the deputies will be back. Maybe you should get Stacy and Pops out of there."

"I already suggested that, but Stacy and Pops refuse to leave. Said they had to stay to take care of the livestock." A hint of humor underscored Marsh's tone. "Stacy has been teaching me about what it takes to run a ranch. I had no idea how much work was involved. Give me a couple of gunmen or an escaped convict any day."

The image of his sister directing Marshall on how to muck stalls made him smile. Yet it also made him feel guilty for dragging Stacy into this. Not that he had had much of a choice, considering how Leanne had shown up at the ranch, bloody and injured.

"Thanks for keeping my family safe," he said humbly. "I owe you big time."

"Nah, you don't owe me anything. I have the cushy job here compared to what you and Jackson have been up against." Marsh's comment made him realize that Jackson must have filled Marsh in on the recent incidents of gunfire. "Hang on, Stacy wants to talk to you."

Before Tuck could protest, he heard his sister's voice on the line. "What's this about you harboring a murder suspect?"

He sighed. "There's more to the story, Stacy, but I don't have time to go into it now. I need you to trust me, okay? I know what I'm doing."

"Do you?" Her tone dripped with skepticism. "I heard this mystery woman of yours is quite the looker."

He tried not to stare at Leanne, but the way she raised her brows indicated she knew he and Stacy were talking about her. He should have figured Pops would mention how pretty Leanne was. Not that it mattered.

He'd have put his life on the line for her no matter what she looked like. Or how old she was. As a cop, he couldn't walk away.

"Don't get yourself killed," Stacy said when he didn't respond. "Pops and I need you." With that, she disconnected the call.

With a sigh, he set the phone on the table. "Sounds like the deputies suspect Leanne is with me," he said to Jackson. "They didn't say that in so many words, as that would have tipped their hand. But if they believe she's with me, we need to fill Captain Owens in on this, sooner than later."

"I'm right here," Leanne said pointedly. "There's no need to talk around me. I'm the one in the middle of this mess."

"Sorry." He sighed. "I should have known the deputies would return to the ranch looking for you. Especially after their attempt to take us out of the picture the following morning failed."

"I'm sure there are only a few bad apples in the bunch." Jackson grimaced. "It's not likely that all of them are dirty. Most cops are doing their best to maintain law and order in the second-largest state in the country. The two that showed up at the ranch might be clean."

He nodded. "I should have asked Marsh for their names. The first two guys who responded were Flores and Lohar. Hard to know if they are involved. All we know for sure is that Dominic is likely one of the bad ones."

Leanne reached for the computer. At first he assumed she was trying to search for more information on Deputy Dominic Clark, but then he saw a different face on the screen.

Her father's obituary.

"I was afraid of this," she whispered, her expression full of anguish. "I had a bad feeling I was all alone in the world."

"You don't know that," he protested, trying to find a way to reassure her.

Tears glistened in her eyes, and she abruptly jumped up and crossed through the connecting doorway. To her credit, she didn't close her side completely, yet it was clear she wanted to be alone.

"What did I miss?" Jackson asked.

"This." Tucker leaned forward to read the details of her father's life and death. The obituary stated Frank was preceded in death by his wife Jean Wolfe, and had dedicated his life to keeping their country safe as a border patrol agent.

That's how Leanne got into the profession. And even more interesting, it appeared her father was killed last year while on the job.

He sat back in his chair, his thoughts whirling. Was Leanne investigating her father's death?

ELEVEN

Leanne buried her face in the pillow as snippets of memories rolled through her mind. Her father smiling and saying how proud he was of her. Then their shared grief over her mother's passing from cancer. And finally, his telling her that he suspected a border patrol agent was looking the other way, allowing certain vehicles to cross the border.

Two weeks later, he and another agent by the name of Robert Homer were found dead, both shot in the chest at close range. There were no witnesses as to what had happened, but she knew her father's murder was related to the human trafficking suspicions he'd shared with her.

She'd asked to be reassigned to his area, but that had taken several months before it was approved. That was why she still had an apartment in Austin. Until then, she'd been working as a liaison with the Austin PD, rather than being assigned to a checkpoint. Once she'd insisted on being transferred, she'd ended up on the midnight shift. She only had two months left on her lease, so she'd been making the long commute, rather than finding a new place to live. Deep down, she'd hoped to give up the checkpoint job once she'd found the man responsible for her father's murder.

Some of the puzzle pieces had fallen into place, but

she needed more. Between her nagging headache and her overwhelming sadness at reliving her father's death, she couldn't think clearly.

Yes, she knew her parents had everlasting life with their Lord Jesus. But she missed them.

"Leanne?" The edge of the mattress dipped as Tucker sat beside her. "Please don't cry."

"I'm not." She sniffled loudly, wiping away her tears. "Okay, I am, but I'm fine."

"I'm sorry," he murmured. "I wish I could make this easier for you."

He was sweet, kind and supportive in a way that touched her heart. She sat up to face him. "Thanks. You should know that I remember asking to be reassigned from my role as a liaison with the Austin PD to the checkpoint my father worked before he was killed."

"So that's why you have an apartment in Austin." Tucker nodded thoughtfully. "I have to admit, that was bugging me."

"Me, too." She tried to smile. "I knew that was a mighty long commute."

"Your goal was to investigate your father's murder." It was a statement, not a question.

"Yes." She shouldn't have been surprised he'd figured that out at the same time she'd remembered. "My dad mentioned he was suspicious of an agent or two letting certain vehicles through. Two weeks later, he and Robert Homer were found dead in their truck, both shot in the chest."

Tucker grimaced. "So rather than taking your suspicions up the chain of command, you asked for a transfer and put yourself in the line of fire."

She hated to admit that when he said it like that, her actions weren't logical. "I didn't know who to trust. And it took a long time for my transfer to be approved, which also made me suspicious." She sighed, tucking her hair behind her ear. "What if my dad's boss was involved?"

"Do you remember his name? That may be a good starting point."

"Santiago Gomez." She was surprised the name flashed in her mind.

"Gomez?" Tucker frowned. "That's the last name of one of the deputies who had lunch at the restaurant across from the Sun Valley Motel."

A shiver snaked down her spine. "The two men could be related."

"We'll check into that. It's a common last name, but the connection is enough to raise my suspicions. This is good work, Leanne. I'm thrilled your memory is starting to return."

"Not all the key information, though." She tried not to sound frustrated. "I guess I expected everything to come back in one fell swoop. Instead, it's like a puzzle piece or two dropping into my lap at a time."

"At this point, I'll take any and all pieces." A smile tugged at the corner of Tucker's mouth. He was so handsome, she had trouble pulling her gaze away. "The picture is already becoming clear. I think whatever you were doing at the checkpoint caused the same guys who killed your father to come after you."

"I think so, too." She wished she could remember why she was near the checkpoint in street clothes, rather than wearing her uniform. And where was her weapon? Had she decided to go undercover? Had she been hiding somewhere, waiting to catch the bad guys in the act?

Had she confronted Troy and someone else, maybe Santiago Gomez, just before Troy had stepped in front of her to take the knife meant for her?

"Leanne." Tucker leaned forward to brush a light kiss on her cheek. "I believe in you."

He'd said those words before, but the way his green eyes radiated warmth made her think he really meant it. Without taking the time to think it through, she moved in to kiss him.

Instantly, heat flared between them. He drew her into his arms, deepening the kiss.

"Tuck?" Jackson called from the adjoining room. Tucker quickly broke off their embrace, his face flushed as he dragged his hand through his sandy hair. "Everything okay?"

"Yes." His husky voice made her smile. She may have initiated the kiss, but he'd been impacted by their embrace, too. To her, he said, "You should come tell Jackson what you remembered."

"Okay." He started to turn away, but she placed her hand on his chest. "I appreciate your support. More than you know."

He briefly covered her hand with his, and they looked at each other for a long moment before he dropped his hand and stepped back. "You—uh, still may be involved with someone. And I—well, my job isn't conducive to relationships."

"I don't think I am involved with anyone, but I understand your point." She hid the stab of disappointment. Clearly Tucker wasn't interested in seeing her again once this was over. "No worries."

He hesitated, as if he was going to say something more, but he didn't. Instead, he stepped across the threshold of their connecting rooms. She followed more slowly, still shaken by his kiss. She didn't need the added complication of a relationship right now, either. Especially since she didn't have all the pertinent bits of her memory to solve this thing. Her feelings for Tucker were real.

Yet that didn't change the facts. She was still a fugitive from justice.

And Tucker and Jackson were harboring a wanted murderer.

He shouldn't have kissed her. Tuck jammed his hands into his pockets, hoping Jackson wouldn't be able to notice how off-balance he felt after that spine-tingling kiss.

When Jackson arched a brow, he winced. So much for not giving away his feelings.

Thankfully, his buddy didn't accuse him of being stupid for getting tangled up with Leanne.

"I think we need to look into my dad's old boss, Santiago Gomez," Leanne said as she joined them. "If he is related to Deputy Gomez, then we may have what we need to get search warrants for their phones, cars and residences."

"You remember your dad's boss? I read the obituary. I'm so sorry for your loss."

"Thank you, Jackson." Leanne glanced at him then quickly looked away. "I remembered a few things, most importantly my dad was also a border patrol agent who told me that he suspected someone within the agency was allowing some vehicles across the border. Two weeks after we had that conversation, my dad and his partner, Robert Homer, were shot and killed."

"That's not a coincidence," Jackson muttered.

"No, it's not." Her eyes flashed—not with grief this time, but anger. "I asked to be transferred to his checkpoint, and that didn't happen for months. I'm not sure why it took so long. I remember my dad's boss, Santiago, coming to the funeral and expressing his condolences." Her eyes narrowed. "Now that I know Deputy Gomez was at the restaurant when they met with the alleged shooter, I think he's involved."

"Speaking of that meeting, Owens never called to let us know if we got a hit in the facial rec system." Tuck pulled out his phone and called his boss. The call went to voicemail, so he left a quick message. "We have new intel and need a name to go with the pictures I sent. Call back ASAP."

"Usually, Owens is on top of things." Jackson frowned. "I hope this isn't a sign that he's taking heat from the governor."

Tuck nodded. "Could be. Especially if the Diamond County sheriff's office is leaning on him. The governor touts his unwavering support of law enforcement officials. I'm sure he would rather hold Leanne in jail while we sort out the details of what happened."

"Maybe I should go off on my own." Leanne frowned. "I hate putting you in this position."

"I'm fine with sticking to you like glue." Tuck glanced at Jackson. "I'll understand if you'd rather walk away."

"And miss all the fun?" Jackson rolled his eyes. "We know more now than we did before. Let's work on finding a connection between Deputy Gomez and Santiago Gomez. That may be the nail we need to convince Owens we're on the right track."

"Okay." The hour was growing late, making him think if they didn't hear from their captain soon, it likely wouldn't be until morning. And maybe that was by design. If the governor had given Owens the directive to bring Leanne in, their boss may be delaying on purpose. "Let's get started."

"What can I do?"

Even with the slight puffiness around her eyes, she was beautiful. He wanted to believe she wasn't like Cherry, that she wouldn't cheat, but it wasn't easy to trust his instincts when it came to women.

And really, Leanne's job as a border patrol agent was not conducive to a long-distance relationship, either. Besides, why did that even matter? He needed to stay focused on finding the dirty cops involved in this thing.

Getting emotionally attached to Leanne was a recipe for disaster. Sam had made that mistake with Mari Lynch and had nearly paid with his life. Although now that Tucker was here with Leanne, he better understood how that had happened.

He'd sacrifice his life for hers, too.

"It's late. I would rather you rest and relax." He smiled. "Your memory is starting to return, and that's the most important thing."

Her expression fell, but she didn't argue. "Will you let me know if you do find a connection between the Diamond County Sheriff's Department and my dad's boss?"

"I promise." He ignored Jackson's knowing smirk. "Get some sleep."

Leanne sighed with disappointment. She reluctantly turned to head back into her room.

"You're in trouble, dude," Jackson said in a low voice so that Leanne couldn't overhear. "So far, we only have her word for what she has and hasn't remembered. She still could be playing us."

He shook his head. "Her grief is real. Besides, there has to be a reason someone is trying to kill her."

"True, but there could be more to the story," Jackson insisted. "You need to think with your brain, not your heart."

"I am." He sat in front of the computer and began a new

search. Thankfully, Jackson took the hint and dropped the issue.

"This would be easier if we knew Deputy Gomez's first name," he muttered as he typed in *Santiago Gomez* and *Diamond County Deputy Gomez*.

Turns out, he didn't need it. The first article that popped up highlighted the brothers fighting crime on the border.

Deputy Thomas Gomez and his older brother, Border Patrol Supervisor Santiago Gomez. And there on the screen was a photograph of the pair smiling broadly for the camera.

"Brothers, huh?" Jackson tapped the image of Deputy Thomas Gomez. "That's definitely the guy at the restaurant. Too bad we don't know more about his other partner, Deputy Barnes."

He had to assume that Barnes was guilty, too. Although, if that was the case, there were an awful lot of dirty cops in this.

Tucker stared at the brothers. "Okay, let's just say these guys are working together, taking money to let certain vehicles through the checkpoint. Maybe those involved in human trafficking. How do Troy Gonzales and Leanne's father fit into the picture? Did they know each other? Was Troy dirty, too, or did he confront Santiago with his suspicions?"

"We won't know that until Leanne's memory returns," Jackson said. "But thinking about how she showed up on your grandfather's ranch wearing street clothes, I think she was doing some undercover work of her own."

He scowled. "I thought you didn't believe her?"

"I never said that," Jackson shot back. "My concern is the way you're getting too involved with her on a personal level. Besides, what I believe isn't the point. It's what we can prove that matters. And right now, we can't prove squat."

"We know Deputy Gomez is the brother of a border patrol agent in a supervisor position." He gestured to the screen. "And that deputy was here in Austin, meeting with a man who escaped when you tried to follow him."

"Yeah, he did." Jackson nodded. "But that's circumstantial at best. We need more." He paused. "Still nothing from Owens?"

"No." The hour was approaching 10:00 p.m. "I doubt we'll hear from him until the morning."

"Maybe we should get some sleep." Jackson yawned. "I'm not sure there's much more we can do without support from our boss."

Since driving out to the Diamond County Sheriff's Department and demanding answers wasn't an option, he was inclined to agree. He reached over and shut the computer. "Okay, we'll sleep on it. And pray that Leanne's memory returns."

"I'm calling first dibs on the bathroom." Jackson rose and headed toward it.

Fifteen minutes later, they were stretched out in their respective beds. Yet despite his bone-weary fatigue—Tucker's day had started early with doing chores on the ranch then getting shot at while in the barn—sleep eluded him.

Partially because memories of Leanne's kiss swirled in his mind. The one he suspected Jackson had witnessed.

Hence the well-deserved lecture. Tuck sighed.

He must have dozed off because a noise pulled him awake. He sat up, listening intently. Jackson was still sleeping, so he'd almost convinced himself that he imagined it when he heard it again.

Thudding noises from somewhere outside. He rose,

reached for his gun, which he'd left on the bedside table, and moved to the window. Their rooms were at the farthest end of the building, and up until now, it had been unusually quiet.

When he looked outside, he froze. The distinctive shape of a police car with high antennas and a light bar stretched across the top was driving along the parking lot. It was too dark to see the writing along the side, but he felt certain the Diamond County deputies had found them.

Maybe even Deputy Gomez himself.

"Jackson," he hissed in a low voice.

His buddy rolled over and squinted at him. Then, sensing his alarm, Jackson sat up and reached for his own gun. "What?"

"We have company." He leaned over to grab the laptop—the only real thing of value, other than their sidearms. "Cops."

"Diamond County?" Jackson moved to join Tucker. "Good thing we parked in back."

"Yeah, but it won't be easy to get out of here without being noticed." He crossed through the connecting doorway. He whispered, "Leanne? Wake up."

"What's wrong?" Her voice was thick with sleep, but like Jackson, she quickly threw back the covers. They were all sleeping in their clothes, which was a good thing now that they needed to get out of there.

Fast.

"There's a squad car outside. We need to get out of here."

"Deputy Gomez?" She ran her fingers through her hair as she stood and jammed her feet into her shoes. "Or Austin PD?"

"Not sure." He gestured to the door. "Your room is closest to the SUV."

"What if he sees us?" Leanne's eyes were wide with apprehension. She glanced from him to Jackson. "They won't hesitate to open fire."

He had the same thought, but they didn't have another option. He glanced at Jackson, who shrugged. "You guys go first. I'll cover you."

"No." He couldn't let his buddy sacrifice his life. "You and Leanne go first." He nodded toward the door. "But hurry. There's no time to waste."

Leanne's eyes filled with distress, but she grabbed the door handle and silently opened it. She peered through the quarter-inch opening. "The cops are roughly sixty yards away. Looks like they're checking out an SUV parked near room five."

Not far enough. He nodded. "Go. Jackson has the keys." When she didn't move, he added, "I'll be right behind you."

She opened the door just wide enough to slip out. Jackson quickly followed her, leaving Tucker to cover their backs. The darkness helped, but as he left the room, taking a moment to close the door softly behind him, he was illuminated in the beam of a spotlight.

The cops had found them!

Holding the computer and Leanne's picture frame he'd grabbed at the last minute up to shield his face, he quickly disappeared around the corner of the building. Jackson already had the SUV engine running, so Tuck didn't hesitate to dive into the back seat.

"Go!" he shouted hoarsely.

Jackson hit the gas, barreling around the back of the motel. By the time Tucker had scrambled into his seat, he looked behind them to see the police vehicle turning the corner.

"Hurry!" he urged, wondering if this was it. The moment they'd all be caught and arrested.

Or worse, shot and killed in one fell swoop. Leaving no witnesses behind.

TWELVE

Hunched in the passenger's seat, Leanne gripped the armrest as Jackson drove around the back of the motel. Adrenaline coursed through her at the thought of the Diamond County deputies finding them. Thankfully, Tucker had made it into the back seat seconds before Jackson peeled away.

"Hurry," Tucker urged again. Jackson hit the gas, sending the car surging forward.

The seat belt tightened painfully against her chest. Lifting her head, she noticed the street ahead was unusually dark. Then she understood Jackson was driving without his headlights.

"Hang on." Jackson took one abrupt turn after another, gunning the engine, then braking to make another turn. The jerky movements made her head pound and nausea churn in her belly.

She kept her head down, even though that only made her feel worse. She thought that maybe if the deputies only saw one person in the vehicle, they'd think they had the wrong one.

Hopefully.

After what seemed like forever, but was probably only ten minutes, the jerky movements stopped. Cautiously, she lifted her head and noticed that Jackson was driving sedately now, with his lights on. Somehow, he'd found a rural highway and was heading away from the city.

"We're clear."

She glanced over her shoulder to find Tucker pushing himself into a sitting position. Then he clicked his seat belt into place. "Nice driving, Jackson."

"That was too close for comfort." Jackson scowled, shaking his head. "I don't like how they found us at the Red Rock Motel. I'm sure Deputy Gomez was likely one of the deputies in the vehicle."

"It could be that they were checking all the smaller motels in the area. If they had known for sure we were there, I doubt we'd be sitting here alive and well."

She shivered at his dire assessment. "Tucker is right. They were looking for signs of us being there. Maybe running license plates to see who owned the vehicles parked in the lot."

"Guess that means we need a new ride," Jackson drawled. "Although we won't be able to rent something now, at four in the morning."

"Agree we need to swap rides." Tucker shrugged. "We'll reach out to Owens in a few hours. For now, keep driving."

"Will do. Maybe we should stay in San Antonio for a while," Jackson said thoughtfully. "It's a big enough city that the deputies wouldn't be able to search every motel to find us."

A memory of the San Antonio riverwalk with its pretty flowers and various restaurants flashed in her mind. She frowned, trying to remember when she'd been there. Recently? With her parents? Or as a child?

The more she tried to recall the outing, the more her head hurt. She gave up, thinking that it was probably better to let the memories come naturally, rather than attempting to force them.

"I like that idea." Tucker nodded. "I'll see what I can come up with."

She settled back against the seat, drawing a deep, shaky breath. Her nerves were just starting to settle when she had another thought. "The deputies must know you're helping me." She turned to look at Tucker, who held out the picture frame of her and her father. Touched that he'd remembered she slid it beneath the front seat to keep it safe. Then turned back to face him. "Do you think they can track your phone?"

Tucker looked up from his phone. "You're probably right that they know I'm helping you. Although if they could track my phone, they'd have found our room without difficulty. Still, it may be worth getting new ones, just in case." His frown deepened. "I wouldn't put anything past these guys. Especially since Santiago Gomez has access to federal resources."

"We'll put that on our list of things to do," Jackson said. "New vehicle, new phones, new place to stay. Anything else?"

Wasn't that enough? Staying one step ahead of the deputies was exhausting.

And they still didn't know exactly what crimes the Gomez brothers were covering up. Something related to illegal border crossings obviously, but that covered a wide range of possibilities.

"Try to get some rest. We'll be on the road for a while."

She grimaced at Tucker, knowing that would be impossible. Now that she was awake, her stomach rumbled with hunger. "Maybe we can stop for breakfast when we get to San Antonio."

"Fine with me," Jackson said.

They fell silent as the SUV ate up the miles between Austin and San Antonio. Jackson didn't go more than five miles over the speed limit so as not to attract undue attention from either the state patrol or other law enforcement agencies. But she kept glancing back to see if anyone was following them.

At this hour, there wasn't much traffic. Which was both good and bad. If the deputies ended up on this highway, they'd be in plain view.

"I found a place that should work." Tucker broke the silence. "It's near the edge of town, but not so rural as to be a draw for the deputies."

"I'm game," Jackson said. "But I don't think we should go there until we have a replacement vehicle and new phones."

"You're right about that." Tucker sighed and scratched his chin. She found his five-o'clock shadow oddly attractive. She forced herself to look away, reminding herself that this was hardly the time to be thinking of kissing him again. "Coffee would be nice, so let's grab breakfast first."

"Works for me." Jackson glanced at her, and she flushed as if he might have read her inappropriate thoughts. "Are you okay?"

"Of course." She ran her fingers through her tangled hair, trying to make herself presentable.

San Antonio was about an hour and a half from Austin, but that was on the interstate. Since Jackson had taken rural highways, the timeframe was longer. It was quarter past six in the morning by the time they reached the outskirts of the city.

Jackson pulled into the parking lot of a family-style restaurant. He turned the vehicle so that they were backed into a space located behind the restaurant, far from any other cars.

She knew without asking that his goal was to provide them with a quick getaway.

It occurred to her that her law enforcement instincts were growing stronger with each passing hour. She prayed that meant her memory would soon return, too.

Ten minutes later, they were settled in a booth near the kitchen. Tucker had indicated she should scoot in first, then dropped onto the bench seat beside her. Jackson took the seat across from them.

A pleasant young woman named Darla Sue brought a pot of coffee.

"Yes, please." Tucker indicated their three empty cups.

"Thank you," Leanne murmured, taking a grateful sip.

Once they'd given their orders, Darla Sue left them alone. Leanne eyed Jackson and Tucker, who seemed lost in thought.

"What is it?" She sensed they were having second thoughts about the proposed plan.

Tucker took a long sip of his coffee, then shrugged. "I was trying to think of a way to set a trap for these guys. All this running and dodging bullets is annoying. I would rather spring a trap and arrest them for doing something illegal."

"I agree, but the problem is that we don't know what they're up to," Jackson protested. He darted a quick glance at her, then added, "At this point, we're the ones harboring a fugitive."

"I know." Tucker stared at his coffee for a moment. "What if we set up a dummy motel room, using one or both of our phones and leaving our current vehicle out front? That might be enough to draw them in."

She was intrigued with the idea. "It will only work if I'm in the room, waiting for them."

Tucker's gaze shot to hers. "No way. That's not happening. I expect they'll burst into the room, guns blazing. If we have a hidden camera inside, getting a video of their faces would be enough to arrest them."

While she was touched by his concern for her well-being, she wasn't sure that his plan would work. "And what if they burst into the room without guns blazing?"

He shrugged, glancing at Jackson. "That wouldn't be great for us. But considering the way they've been taking shots at every turn, I suspect they'll go in hot and heavy."

"It could work," Jackson agreed.

She nodded. "Okay. I'm in." At this point, it was worth a try. Because like Tucker, she was getting tired of being on the run.

And she had to accept the possibility her memory may not return in time to be of any use in solving this thing.

Tucker was glad to have a plan. Especially one that wouldn't put Leanne in harm's way.

He couldn't believe she'd suggested waiting in the motel room for the deputies to break down the door.

Their server arrived with their breakfasts. She topped off their coffee mugs. "Do you'all need anything else?"

"No thanks." Jackson smiled.

After Darla Sue left, Tuck was surprised when Leanne grasped his hand beneath the table.

"I'd like to say grace." She bowed her head. "Dear Lord Jesus, we ask You to bless this food and to continue keeping us all safe in Your care. Amen."

"Amen," he and Jackson echoed. As before, Tuck felt the impact of the prayer in a new way.

As if God really was watching over them.

They ate for a few minutes until Jackson broke the silence. "We'll need to call Owens about the motel room idea. I don't think we should try to pull that off without approval."

Tuck grimaced. The problem with asking permission is the possibility of their boss saying no. "Might be easier to ask for forgiveness later." He gave a lopsided smile.

Jackson shrugged. "That's up to you."

"Don't get in trouble on my account." Leanne frowned. "I don't want to be responsible for one of you losing your job."

"I doubt it will come to that," Tucker assured her. "We've gotten good results over the past few cases we've worked. The goal is always to put the bad guys behind bars. This might be a case where the ends justify the means."

Jackson grunted without saying anything more.

As Tucker pulled cash from his pocket to pay the bill, Jackson said, "We won't be able to buy replacement phones or a camera for another two hours. The store doesn't open until nine o'clock."

He grimaced, realizing Jackson was right. It was too early to put their plan in motion. "Okay, we have a few hours to kill. I'm open to ideas."

"How close are we to the riverwalk?"

"You want to play tourist?" He looked at Leanne, surprised.

"No, I just have a vague memory of the place." She flushed. "Could be nothing. It is a local attraction. But maybe walking along the river will spur another memory."

"It can't hurt," Jackson agreed. "And if it doesn't work, we can go from there to the closest store to get our supplies."

After a moment's hesitation, Tucker nodded. "Okay. We're a few miles from the riverwalk, so we'll need to find a place to park that's a little closer."

"Thanks." Leanne's blue eyes reflected gratitude. "It's driving me insane that I can't remember when I've been here before."

He told himself not to get too excited. This outing wasn't likely to jog her memory, just like the trip to her apartment.

They found a parking lot not far from the riverwalk. He glanced at Jackson. "Let's power down the phones and leave them under the seat."

"Good idea." Jackson pulled his phone out and complied with the plan.

As they headed toward the winding walkway that lined the river on both sides, Tucker had to resist glancing over his shoulder. They were vulnerable, being out in the open like this. Yet, he also knew this was the last place the deputies would bother to look for them.

He and Jackson kept Leanne between them. He noticed she looked around curiously, and he wondered if she'd been there with her parents at some point.

"If we're going to set up a motel room as bait, we may need to return to Austin." He glanced at Jackson. "Maybe the other side of the city? Unless you think that staying that close will be too obvious."

"I think that's the most logical place they'd look for us. Especially if they keep searching motels for us the way they did this morning."

He knew what Jackson meant. "I know. I considered the possibility they'll try something different after losing us at the Red Rock Motel. I hope leaving the phones on in the room will work."

Jackson nodded. He knew his buddy was thinking the

same thing he was. Their attempt to lure the deputies in may not yield anything.

Then again, it wasn't like they had a better option.

Leanne abruptly stopped. He and Jackson both took another step before turning to face her. Her gaze was fixated on a restaurant up ahead. The exterior was not that unique, but there were several brightly colored umbrellas topping tables outside. At this hour they were empty, but he knew they'd be full of tourists later.

Well, as many tourists that came to Texas while the daytime temperatures were still so hot.

"We ate lunch there." She gestured toward the place. "We sat under the pink umbrella."

"Go on," he urged, tamping down a surge of excitement. "Do you remember anything else?"

She nodded slowly. "My dad told me to be careful. This is where we were when he told me that he suspected someone within the border patrol was allowing vehicles to pass through illegally." She frowned. "Although I don't remember why we came out here for that conversation when I was living in Austin."

"That's great that you're starting to remember." He smiled encouragingly. "Did your dad live in San Antonio? Or maybe a town south of city? Maybe this was the halfway spot for you to get together."

Her eyes lit up. "Uvalde! My dad lived in Uvalde!" She gestured to the restaurant. "This would be a good halfway point for us to meet. And a neutral location, too."

"Do you remember your dad's address?" He kept his tone casual. Her dad had been gone long enough that someone else would probably have either bought or rented the place, but he was curious to at least check it out. "Maybe he left something behind that would help us?"

She scrunched her forehead. "I believe he lived in an apartment, but I doubt he left anything useful behind. I must have taken his belongings with me after he died." She frowned. "There were some boxes in my closet back at the apartment. I didn't even think about the possibility they might contain my dad's things."

"Okay, that's fine. It's not like we would have had time to grab the boxes on our way out of there." Although, it would be interesting to head back there at some point to go through them. "Can you remember anything else?"

Scanning the riverwalk, she slowly shook her head. "No. Sorry. But I'm glad we came here."

He was, too. Glancing at his watch, he realized they'd burned nearly an hour walking around the place. "I say we head back to Austin, since that's where we're going to set the trap. By the time we get there, the stores will be open."

"Let's do it." Jackson seemed as eager as he was to put their plan in motion.

Leanne shot one last look at the bright umbrellas before turning to join them. He wished she had remembered more, like where they might find proof of the Gomez brothers being dirty, but resigned himself to the fact that likely wouldn't happen.

Better they move forward with the plan of setting a trap for the deputies.

Jackson stopped at the local gas station to fill up the tank before they made the drive back to Austin. They used the interstate this time, and there was more than enough traffic to provide a sense of anonymity.

When they reached Austin, the hot sun was in full force. As they pulled into the parking lot, the big box store was open.

"Perfect timing." Jackson grinned.

The phones were easy to pick out, but the camera setup

took more time. They needed one with software to link to their new phones, so they could record when and if the deputies showed up to arrest—or, more likely, kill—Leanne.

When they had what they needed, the total bill was staggering. He hesitated, glancing at Jackson. "I don't have enough cash. I'll have to use a credit card."

"I'll use mine," his buddy offered. "They may not know for sure that I'm involved. If I were in their shoes, I'd focus my efforts and resources on you."

"Thanks. You know I'll reimburse you."

Jackson waved that off and quickly paid for the equipment. Soon, they were back on the road heading to the northwest side of Austin. The Willow Brook Motel he'd found was very similar to both Sun Valley and Red Rock. He hoped that would be another draw for the deputies.

When he approached the front desk, the clerk looked surprised by his request for a room. "Check-in time isn't for hours yet."

"I'll pay extra." He flashed his badge. "It's important."

"Why not? We're not fully booked anyway," the clerk agreed.

That gave him pause. "Can we have a room that's isolated from those that are occupied?"

The clerk nodded. "Fine with me." He took the cash and passed a room key across the counter. "You'all have a nice day."

Tucker nodded and headed back outside. He gestured to the room near where he wanted Jackson to park. "The rooms on either side of this one are empty, too."

Jackson grunted his approval as they headed inside to get to work.

Getting the new phones connected with the two cameras didn't take as long as Tuck feared. When that was finished, he glanced around the room. "Now we need a good place to hide them. Somewhere they won't be damaged by gunfire."

"The top of that mirror. And maybe along the upper edge of the molding above the bathroom door."

He nodded at Leanne and set about getting the small cameras mounted in those two locations. Stepping back, he took a moment to admire his work. The small cameras weren't invisible, but it would take time for someone to notice them. Especially if the persons involved were focused on finding Leanne there.

The trap was set. All they needed was for the rat to come and take the cheese.

THIRTEEN

Leanne watched as Tucker plugged his original phone into a charger and set it on the bedside table. After making sure it was powered up, he stepped back. "Okay. I think we're ready. I'd like to leave the SUV here, but we need to arrange for a rental, first."

"Hang on." Jackson was working his phone. "I found a place that isn't far from here. We can get there and back in roughly forty minutes. I doubt our perps will show up during that time frame." After a brief hesitation, he set his phone down next to Tucker's. "I'll leave this behind, too."

For the first time since she'd shown up on Tucker's grandfather's ranch, she felt as if they were getting close to ending this thing. She would rather be stationed in the motel room waiting for the deputies to arrive, but having cameras was the next best thing. Since they'd been found at the Red Rock Motel, it stood to reason the deputies would eventually find the SUV outside the Willow Brook Motel, too.

Especially if they were able to track Tucker's phone.

Based on the access Santiago Gomez had within his role with the Department of Homeland Security, she expected him to work on that very soon. If he hadn't done so already.

Thinking of Santiago made her wonder how she'd manage to go back to work as a border patrol agent if her memory didn't return. A flash of panic hit hard, but she did her best to shrug it off. No point in worrying about that now. Once they'd arrested the dirty cops involved in this mess, she could see a doctor for treatment options.

If there were any.

Before they could leave, Tucker's phone rang. They froze, glancing at each other in alarm, even though it wasn't likely the caller would be either of the Gomez brothers. Tucker quickly crossed over to look at the screen. "Owens."

"Go ahead." Jackson waved a hand. "May as well fill him in."

Leanne listened to Tucker's side of the conversation with his boss. First, he discussed their suspicions about Deputy Thomas Gomez, who could be working with his older brother, Santiago Gomez—a supervisor with the border patrol. He explained about how they had been found at the Red Rock Motel by two deputies in a squad car, but had managed to escape. He also outlined their plan to set a trap for the deputies.

"I understand this may not work," Tucker said, after listening for a minute. "But we're running out of options. We don't have anything concrete against either Gomez brother. For all we know, they truly believe Leanne is guilty."

What? She scowled, but Tucker raised a hand, indicating he was just appeasing his boss.

"You got a hit?" Tucker's voice rose with excitement. "That's great! What's his name?"

It took Leanne a moment to remember the photograph Jackson had taken of the deputies meeting with an unknown male. It seemed like so much had happened since then, but really it was only yesterday.

"Kurt-with-a-*K* Watkins," Tucker repeated for their benefit. "And he's in the system because he was arrested for possession of an illegal firearm?"

Gun trafficking? She frowned. She couldn't remember what she'd been working on, or what her father had suspected, but that didn't seem right. Not that guns couldn't be brought across the border, but her gut instincts were telling her that this was either about people or drugs.

Maybe both.

Jackson had crossed over to pick up his phone. After a few minutes, he nodded with satisfaction. "That's the guy," he said softly for Tucker's benefit. He flashed the picture for her to see, too. "I'm sure of it."

"Thanks, boss. We'll keep you in the loop. Oh, make a note of our temporary numbers." Tucker rattled off the information. "Yep, I got it."

"Sounds like your boss is on board with your plan," she said when he'd ended the call.

"He is." Tucker grinned. "Took a little smooth talking on my part, as you heard. But discovering the family relationship between Thomas and Santiago Gomez convinced him we may be onto something." His expression turned somber. "He's been tied up for a while because the governor has been giving him a hard time. Owens is being pressured to use Texas Ranger resources to bring you in. We're often assigned to pursue fugitives from justice."

She winced, even though she'd known it was just a matter of time. "How long do we have?"

He shrugged. "Boss didn't say anything specifically, but obviously, the sooner we crack this thing, the better." He gave the motel room one last glance. "I really hope this works."

"Me, too." She followed Tucker and Jackson out to the SUV. As Jackson had promised, the rental facility was fifteen minutes away. There was a slight delay as the representative had to find a black SUV, but finally they located one. Jackson insisted on putting the vehicle under his name.

"It may not give us much time." His tone was low so only she and Tucker could hear. "But I don't see another option."

"We should have asked your boss to put it in his name," she said, only half joking.

Tucker lifted a shoulder. "I'm sure it will be fine. If the trap works, they won't have a reason to go looking for a second vehicle."

"Okay." She forced a smile even though it wasn't easy to shake off the feeling of apprehension. It was one thing to know that she was the one being targeted.

She hated the idea of Tucker or Jackson being in the line of fire, too.

"I need a gun." The statement popped out of her mouth before she could think it through. But now that the idea had come to her, she wondered why she hadn't thought of it sooner.

Both guys looked at her in shock. Jackson handed Tucker the keys to the rental, giving him an arched look that indicated he didn't want to be in the middle of this discussion. "Take the replacement vehicle. I'll grab your SUV and meet you back at the Willow Brook Motel."

"Thanks, Jackson." Tucker waited until his buddy loped away before opening the passenger door for her. "I'm not sure that's a good idea."

"Of course it is," she shot back. "We know I was a border patrol agent, so I'm pretty sure I'll remember how to use it."

His jaw clenched. He didn't say anything, but closed her door and went around to get behind the wheel. For several long minutes, neither of them broke the silence. But then she caught a glimpse of a sporting goods store. She grabbed his arm. "Look, that place will have guns."

"You don't have an ID," he protested.

She shot him an exasperated look. "You can buy it for me. I promise I won't use it unless we're physically threatened."

He shook his head, driving straight past the store. "I'll think about it. For now, we need to pick up Jackson."

She scowled and crossed her arms over her chest. She didn't understand his reluctance to provide her with a weapon. They had possibly three deputies—Dominic Clark, Deputy Barnes and Thomas Gomez—Border Patrol Agent Santiago Gomez, this new player Kurt Watkins and the shooter in the silver truck working against them.

Even if she was armed, they were still outnumbered.

Was it possible Tucker still didn't trust her?

She glanced over, taking in his stern profile. Yeah, maybe that was the real issue. He was willing to put his life on the line to protect her and to work the case, but he didn't really trust her.

Turning away, she stared blankly out the passenger window, her heart aching with the realization that her feelings for Tucker were one-sided. Despite their kiss, he didn't care for her on a personal level. Once they had the bad guys in jail, she'd never see him again.

In that moment, she felt keenly alone.

Obviously, Leanne was upset with him. Tucker could feel her anger radiating off her in waves. He hated feeling like a jerk. Was he being unreasonable? He had given her the shotgun for protection when they were back at the ranch, but this was different.

Wasn't it?

Not really. He tried not to groan as he fought the urge to turn around. He wanted to talk this through with Jackson first, even though his buddy had gotten out of there as if his backside were on fire.

Logically, it made some sense to even the odds. Still, he didn't want to imagine what would happen if she was forced to use the weapon, if only in a clear case of self-defense. After all, she was wanted for murder.

He missed the next turn and was forced to backtrack. He watched the rearview mirror, grateful that no one appeared to be following them.

His new phone chirped. Pulling it from his pocket, he expected to see Owens's number, since his boss was the only one who had the information.

It took him a minute to recognize Marsh's number. He quickly answered, using the speaker function while driving. "Hey, Marsh. Did you get this number from the boss?"

"Yep." There was a slight pause before Marsh continued. "I thought you should know the deputies came back for round two bright and early this morning." His fellow Ranger got straight to the point. "They bluntly told us they have reason to believe you're hiding Leanne Wolfe and that you'll be facing charges of aiding and abetting a criminal if you don't turn her over to the Diamond County Sheriff's Department ASAP."

He glanced at Leanne, who was clearly listening. "That's interesting, considering we barely evaded two deputies searching the Red Rock Motel parking lot last night. Let me guess. Their names are Gomez and Barnes?"

"Yep. I'm glad you were able to get away, but it sounds like you're on their radar," Marsh said. "Your sister is worried about you."

"Tell Stacy I'm fine. Sounds to me as if they're feeling

desperate." Not to mention setting the stage so that they have reason to shoot him and Leanne together. "Did they say anything about Jackson?"

"No, and I didn't tell them who I was, either," Marsh said. "I pretended to be Stacy's husband. They didn't seem to care about us. They're laser-focused on finding you."

"Okay. I already assumed I was on their radar, and this just confirms that. I really need you to keep Pops and my sister safe. I'm worried that if they don't find me soon, they'll come back to the ranch to make life miserable for the two of them."

"Of course I'll keep them safe. Although I don't think Gomez and Barnes will be back here anytime soon." A hint of humor underscored Marsh's voice. "Pops threatened them with the shotgun if they returned."

Tuck swallowed a groan. "Of course he did."

"I did my best to smooth things over. I reassured the deputies that you were smart enough not to come back to the ranch," Marsh went on. "And Stacy mentioned that the two of you took turns spending time there. Hopefully, we bought you and Jackson a little time. But it's obvious they're gearing up to take you and Leanne down."

"Yeah. I hear you." He could feel Leanne glaring at him, but ignored it. "Thanks again, Marsh."

"Stay safe, Tuck. You, too, Leanne." With that, Marsh ended the call.

"Don't say it." He held up his hand, sensing she was about to insist he buy her a gun. "We need to meet Jackson at the motel. From there, we'll decide our next steps."

"Okay. But keep in mind that I'm the target." She didn't look happy. "Do you think I like knowing you and Jackson could end up as collateral damage?"

"We can take care of ourselves." As he said the words,

he realized the same was likely true for her. Maybe she had shown up bruised, bloody and seemingly defenseless at the ranch, but that's because she was either a victim or a witness to a crime.

"Famous last words," she muttered.

At her pointed look, he sighed and nodded. "We'll work on getting you armed once we're far away from the motel."

"Thank you." Her voice was low and husky. It shouldn't have made him think about kissing her again, but it did.

Who was the idiot now?

He concentrated on getting back to the Willow Brook Motel. Seeing Jackson had parked his SUV directly outside their room, he pulled into a spot several spaces down.

Jackson must have been watching for them, because he opened the door before he could knock. "One of the cameras fell down, but I was able to get it back up. Let's test it to make sure it's working."

Tucker pulled out his phone. "Jump up and down."

Jackson did so, and the phone screen lit up with an image of Jackson's jumping. He realized he hadn't set an audible alarm, so he took the time to do that now.

"It works." He tucked the phone in his pocket. "Marsh called. Our famous deputy duo showed up on the ranch this morning to put my sister and Pops on notice that they're looking for me, as they believe I'm hiding Leanne. They're threatening to arrest me as I'm aiding and abetting a criminal." He gestured to the room. "I have a good feeling about this. The search for us is heating up. I think it's only a matter of time before they show up here."

"Let's go." Jackson pulled the door open. Tucker's phone dinged as they left. Their walking out had triggered the camera.

"Grab the laptop," Tucker said as they walked past his SUV.

"Wait, I need my picture frame, too," Leanne said. "Should I leave your grandfather's phone in here, Tucker?"

"Yes, please."

She nodded and removed her photo from beneath the seat as Jackson retrieved the computer. Good thing he'd brought it with him when they'd bolted from the Red Rock Motel.

"I thought we were going to discuss our next steps," Leanne said as they piled into the rental. He took the laptop from Jackson and slid it under his seat. "Maybe the trap will work, and I truly hope it does. But if not, I need to be armed so that I can help back you up."

Jackson kept his eyes straight ahead. Tucker wanted to punch him, but settled for saying, "Jackson, you get a vote in this, too."

"Great, that makes me the tiebreaker." Jackson sighed. "I'm not opposed to the idea of giving Leanne a gun. It will get messy if she's forced to use it, since it won't be registered under her name. Yet if that happens, then it only proves her point. That it was a good idea to give her a weapon in the first place. Besides, I don't trust those deputies as far as I can throw them. I wouldn't put it past them to play dirty."

He made several good points. "Okay, then we'll do it." He caught Leanne's relieved expression and grimaced. "Good thing I didn't spend all our cash reserves at the big box store."

"I know where we can buy a gun," Jackson said. "It's on the other side of the city, though."

"Works for me." He drummed his fingers on the armrest. "Once we're settled, we need to see if we can find a connection between Kurt Watkins and our deputies. Or Santiago Gomez. Other than the photo you took of them having lunch," he added. "They could easily claim that was a casual encounter."

"It seems more likely that Watkins is a hired gun for them." Leanne looked thoughtful. "And their meeting was to strategize how to track us down. Too bad he's not the same guy we saw in the silver truck."

"I know, but if we dig through the police files and find pictures of some of Watkins's known associates, I may be able to recognize the gunman." He tried not to get too depressed about their lack of progress. "Not that I expect that to be easy."

"Finding known associates would help," Jackson agreed.

Tucker's phone chimed. Excitedly, he pulled it from his pocket. The picture on the screen confused him, because the motel room was empty. He backed up the short video and noticed a vehicle had driven past the room.

"Pull over," he told Jackson. "We have movement outside our room."

"Already?" Jackson didn't stop until the next intersection, then he drove up into the parking lot of a law office. "That was quick."

"It could be nothing," Tucker warned, still watching the screen. "The camera along the top of the bathroom doorframe caught movement outside the room. Either a car or a person walking by. I can't tell because there's a bit of a glare from the sun." *Something I should have tested.* What if the two cameras they'd put in position weren't enough? "No one has tried to get inside the room yet."

Everyone fell silent, waiting for something to happen. The minutes passed slowly, until Jackson finally said, "False alarm. It is a motel. There's likely to be more of people or cars going by."

"Yeah." Disappointed, he glanced up from the screen.

"Let's go. We need to get that weapon, then find a place to stay."

Jackson pulled back out into traffic. When he reached the store that had bars on the windows and was clearly a gun store, he killed the engine. "I'll buy it. Wait here."

Tucker dug cash from his pocket and thrust it toward him. "Not sure how much you'll need."

"No need. I know the guy who owns the place. He'll give me a deal." Jackson slid out and headed inside.

"I appreciate you trusting me like this," Leanne said when they were alone. "I know it's not easy for you to believe me."

"That's not the problem." He twisted in his seat to face her. "You'll get in more trouble than you're already in if you shoot one of those deputies."

"So will you. Besides, I'm praying it won't come to that."

It didn't take Jackson long to get the weapon. When he returned, he tossed what appeared to be a basic .38 with a box of ammo in the back seat for Leanne.

Tucker turned to watch her examine the gun. She handled it like an expert, reminding him of how she'd done the same thing with the shotgun. With a nod, she set the clip and put a round in the chamber. "Looks great, Jackson. Thanks."

"You're welcome." A hint of a smile tugged at his buddy's lips.

Tucker's phone chirped again. With a sigh, he picked it up. Maybe they shouldn't have aimed the camera directly at the main door and the window. He watched the video for a moment without seeing anything.

Without warning, as there was no sound, bullets punctured the door and shattered the window. He blinked then watched in shock and horror as a seemingly endless stream of bullets came toward the camera, bits of plaster and dust filling the air.

The trap had been sprung, but not in the way he'd hoped. The deputies, if they were the ones involved, were recklessly pummeling the room with gunfire.

With the clear intent to kill everyone inside.

FOURTEEN

"What's going on?" Leanne noticed the color leeching from Tucker's face as he stared at the phone. "Did someone get inside the motel room?"

"Not exactly." He sighed. "Bullets are ripping through the room."

Bullets? She instinctively glanced down at the new weapon Jackson had gotten for her. "That's it? The cameras didn't pick up any people?"

"No." He tossed the phone to her. "And the cameras are out of commission now anyway. I saved the video that initially came through. See for yourself."

With shaky fingers, she played with the video feed on the small screen. She replayed from the beginning, and gasped out loud when she saw the bullets piercing the door and shattering the window. Drywall dust and plaster filled the air. She'd lost count of how many bullets had entered the room when suddenly the camera feed went black.

"I can't believe it." The images sent her inwardly reeling. If she had been inside the room, there was no question she'd have been killed.

Tucker and Jackson, too.

Jackson executed an abrupt U-turn.

"Where are you going?" she asked.

"We need to head back to the motel." Jackson's expression was grim. "This is going to hit the news, and that vehicle outside the motel room is registered to Tucker."

Based on how the bullets had torn through the room, she had to assume similar gunfire had severely damaged Tucker's SUV.

"This is bad," she whispered.

"Yeah." Tucker sounded upset. "The rooms on either side of us were empty, but we need to make sure no one was hurt."

She handed the phone back to him, the video images seared into her mind. "I can't believe they hit the room so soon after we left the phones there, and in broad daylight." Then she brightened. "Someone will have seen the vehicle. There may be outside cameras that captured the license plate."

"I should have set up a third camera outside the room," Tucker said with disgust.

"Not your fault." She reached over to lightly touch his shoulder. "Most motels have at least one camera near the lobby." The brief memory of using one of those videos to identify a suspect flashed in her mind. Obviously, she'd done that before. Once again, she wished more pertinent memories would spring forth rather than oddball snippets of her work life. She pushed that aside. "All we need is one snapshot of the license plate. If we can link the total annihilation of the motel room to the Diamond County Sheriff's Department, we'll have probable cause to arrest them."

"As cops, they'll have covered their tracks. The only thing we can hope for is that they're desperate enough to have made a mistake."

Tucker sounded so upset and dejected, her heart ached for him. "It was a good plan," she said softly. "We couldn't have anticipated they'd shoot the place up like something out of the Old West."

"Yeah." He turned to look back at her. "One thing for sure, there's no mistaking the fact that these guys wanted you dead."

"I know." She swallowed hard. Seeing the bullets that had been meant for her was unnerving. "I'm glad you talked me out of staying inside."

"Hear those sirens?" Jackson met her gaze in the rearview mirror. "Local police are heading to the scene."

She understood his warning. She was wanted for murder, and they were going to be surrounded by cops any minute. She hesitated, unsure what to do. "You should drop me off someplace."

"No," Tucker said firmly. "My SUV is the one outside the motel room. Jackson, you need to drop me off and stay with Leanne. Maybe drive around a bit, see if you can find any sign of the deputies."

She wanted to protest, but it made more sense for Tucker to be the one to show up at the motel. Then she frowned. "Wait, what if they arrest you?"

"Leanne is right. You can't go." Jackson turned into a gas station parking lot. "I'll head over and explain how I borrowed your car. I'll claim I rented the room for a friend who hasn't arrived yet." He shrugged. "I will vouch for the fact that I haven't seen you and that I have no idea who would have wanted to shoot up the motel room."

She found herself holding her breath as she waited for Tucker's response. Finally, he nodded.

"Okay. You go," Tucker agreed. "Let us know if you find any information that will help us nail these guys."

"Will do." Jackson thrust some cash at him, dropped the key fob into the cup holder in the center console then slid out from behind the wheel. "Fill up the tank. I have a feeling this is going to be a long day."

"Truth," she said as he slammed the door shut. She reached for the gun and tucked it into her waistband, pulling the edge of her black shirt down to cover it. She got out of the car to sit up front with Tucker.

His expression was somber as he headed inside to pay with cash, then began to fill the tank. She stood beside him, welcoming the shade. He appeared to be lost in thought, and none of it good.

"This isn't your fault. These guys are escalating."

He glanced at her and nodded. "That is worrisome. I'm appalled at how they don't seem to care how many innocent people they hurt along the way."

Once the tank had been topped off, they hit the road. Tucker chose a road that ran parallel to the motel. She could see dozens of red-and-blue flashing lights, but he made sure to stay off to the side.

After passing the motel, they headed away from Austin on a long and winding highway. She wasn't sure what destination Tucker had in mind, other than staying off the radar.

He watched the rearview mirror often. Up ahead, there was a junction with another highway, and he turned left in the general direction of Austin. She frowned. "Why are you heading back to the city?"

"We'll need to pick Jackson up sooner or later." He glanced at her. "I'm mostly just cruising the highways to see if the deputies or our shooter happen to be hanging out nearby."

That made sense. "If Gomez and Barnes are nearby, they could be listening in on the radio channel to learn information."

"Exactly." He grimaced. "Makes me wish I'd thought

of purchasing a two-way radio when we stopped for the phones and cameras."

Since there was nothing they could do about that now, she shrugged. "I like Jackson's story about how he'd borrowed your car and is meeting up with a friend at the motel, but he's going to have a tough time explaining away the cameras." She winced. "I guess he could claim that someone else must have put them there."

"That won't work if they're processed for prints." Tucker smacked the steering wheel, his features full of self-disgust. "Man, I totally botched this. I thought we'd have camera footage showing the shooter as they breached the door and that we'd arrest them."

"You need to stop beating yourself up." She put a hand on his arm. "We're human. We make mistakes. Jackson and I both thought the plan would work. The blame lies with all of us, not just you."

He sighed. "It's nice of you to try to make me feel better. From here on out, we can't underestimate these guys. It's not good that they're staying one step ahead of us."

"I think this is a huge mistake on their part. They shot an empty room, exposing themselves in the middle of the day where someone likely saw what happened."

"You're right. That's a good way to look at this." He surprised her by covering her hand with his and squeezing gently. "Thanks."

"Anytime." She hoped he didn't notice the slight hitch in her voice. Tucker's sweet side was going to be the death of her.

She already liked him more than she should.

Tucker glanced at the clock for the tenth time in ten minutes. He really wanted to call Jackson, to hear what—

if anything—his buddy had discovered, but tried to remain patient. It might take Jackson some time to get answers, especially since he was technically a victim.

When he was still several miles outside of Austin, he decided that driving aimlessly wasn't helpful. To conserve fuel, he pulled off the road and parked near a pair of scraggly looking trees.

"I'm sure Jackson is being interrogated." Leanne sighed. "I was hoping we'd have heard something by now."

"Me, too." He pushed out of the driver's side door while she exited on her side. "You may have guessed that patience isn't my strong suit."

"Mine either." She frowned. "At least from what I can tell."

He eyed her curiously. "No new memories, huh?"

"Nothing useful." She lowered herself to the ground at the base of one of the trees and hugged her knees. "I've been praying that my memories will return in time to be of use."

Maybe he should pray for the same thing. He'd accepted Mari's and Sam's Christian beliefs at face value without really taking them to heart. Meanwhile, Leanne was constantly praying, despite not being able to remember her past.

He dropped down beside her. "I'm sure you'll remember soon."

"I keep going back to the night I approached your grandfather's house. No phone. No gun. No ID or cash." She touched the cross necklace at her neck. "Nothing but this gold cross."

Not to mention the blood. He held her gaze. "You looked as if you'd been running for some time."

She nodded. "The more I think about it, the more I believe the dream I had of Troy Gonzales stepping in front of me to keep me from being stabbed is real. And that incident must have happened relatively close to the ranch."

That was an interesting angle to consider. "There are some canyons on the far south side of the property." He envisioned the area in his mind. The old service road where he'd seen the black pickup driving away was in the same general direction. Maybe there was another road back there that he wasn't aware of? "And those canyons are approximately fifteen to twenty miles from the border."

She turned to look at him. "If we don't come up with any other leads, we should head back there. Maybe seeing the canyons will help me recall what I might have been doing there."

"It's possible, but the deputies may have someone watching the ranch." It's what he would do if the situation was reversed. "We'll have to approach from a different angle."

"Okay." She looked relieved. "It's always important to find the original scene of the crime."

"Spoken like a true investigator," he said lightly.

His phone rang. Seeing Jackson's number on the screen, he didn't hesitate to answer. "What's going on?"

"The good news is that no one was hurt," Jackson said in a hushed tone. "Your car is a wreck, and so is the motel room. The gunman managed to keep any rounds from striking the rooms on either side, which confirms the target was that room specifically, not a random attack."

Tuck was relieved that no one was hurt. "We knew that much. Anything else? Did they find the cameras?"

"Not yet, but the crime scene techs are on the way." Jackson's voice dropped even lower, making it hard to hear. "I may have to admit to having placed them there."

"My prints are on them, too. Maybe you should get out of there before they can arrest you."

"I had the same thought. I'll head out soon and let you know when and where to pick me up. But the main reason I'm calling is that there was camera video from the front lobby. A black pickup truck with tinted windows rolled past three times. After the third time, the clerk said he heard the multiple rounds of gunfire."

"License plate?"

"Nope. Blacked out with mud. And no image of the driver's face either, thanks to the tinted windows. Local cops are still canvassing the area for witnesses. The clerk told the cops he'd rented that room to a Texas Ranger."

"Great." Tucker rested his head back against the tree trunk, staring up at the puffy clouds in the sky. "Every cop in the entire state will be looking for me."

"I told them I obtained the room," Jackson said. "But I can tell they suspect something more is going on."

Tucker was silent for a moment. "Sounds like we have nothing more than what we already know. A driver of a black pickup truck with tinted windows sprayed the motel room with bullets and got away clean."

"Yup." There was a pause, then Jackson hurriedly said, "Gotta go," and ended the call.

"No license plate?" Leanne asked. "Seriously?"

"We knew they'd cover their tracks." He tucked his phone back in his pocket. "I figured the vehicle used by the shooter would either be the black or silver truck." He thought back to the brief glimpse he'd gotten of the driver of the silver truck. "I don't remember the silver truck having tinted windows, do you?"

"No, I don't." Leanne frowned. "And I think we'd have noticed. At the time we passed the truck, it seemed to be simply ambling along. There was nothing to alert us that a gunman was behind the wheel waiting to shoot."

"Yeah. I thought the guy would be an older rancher, but couldn't have been more wrong." He rose to his feet and offered her his hand to help her up. "Come on. We should head back to Austin. If Jackson can avoid being arrested over this, he'll need us to pick him up."

She took his hand and levered herself up. For a moment, they stood staring at each other beneath the shade of the tree. She looked tired and stressed, yet so very beautiful it made his heart ache.

His gaze dropped to her mouth, and she moved toward him. "Tucker," she whispered, her husky voice giving him chills. He loved the way she said his name.

Logically, he knew he shouldn't be doing this. Shouldn't even think of seeing Leanne again once this nightmare was over. But all rational thought vanished when she lifted up on her tiptoes to kiss him.

He drew her close, reveling in their embrace. Somehow, their second kiss packed even more of a punch. When she wrapped her arms around his neck, he nearly groaned.

Two shots of gunfire rang out.

Instantly, he broke off from their kiss and dropped to the ground, pulling Leanne with him. He reached for his weapon and noticed she'd done the same. He couldn't deny being glad she was armed, too.

By tacit agreement, they positioned themselves so their backs were pressed together as they huddled at the base of the two trees.

"Where's the shooter?" He scanned the desolate area around them. "I don't see anything." He'd chosen a rather isolated spot to wait. There wasn't a car or house nearby. Or any other places to hide.

"I don't see anything either," Leanne admitted. Then she turned to glance at him. "If you ask me, the gunshot sounded as if it came from that way." She gestured to the south. "I don't think we were the target. The gunshot was too far away to have struck either of us."

She was right. His reaction had been instinctive, mostly because they'd been targeted by gunfire more times than he could count. But replaying the moment the gunshot had rang out, he realized it had come from a distance.

He jumped to his feet, and once again offered his hand. "We need to check it out."

Leanne didn't hesitate to agree. They hurried to the rental and climbed inside. The interior was stifling hot, so he cranked the air and opened the windows.

He made a three-point turn in the road to go south, away from Austin. He pulled out his phone and handed it to Leanne. "Hold this in case Jackson calls or we need to alert the authorities."

"What do you think we'll find?" Trepidation lined her voice. "I was hoping someone shot a deer or a coyote."

"It's not hunting season," he pointed out. "But maybe if a car struck a deer, the driver would shoot it to put the animal out of its misery."

Yet deep down, he didn't believe it. Maybe he was overreacting, but he felt certain the weapon was used against a person.

An innocent victim, like maybe a carjacking or a domestic dispute? Or a not-so-innocent victim, like one drug dealer taking out another?

He drove slowly, carefully scanning the terrain. "Let me know if you see anything unusual out your side."

"Of course." She swept her gaze over the area, too. After a mile passed, she looked at Tucker. "Is that a vehicle up ahead?"

"Maybe." They were too far away to tell for sure. He

approached with caution, looking for anyone running or driving away.

But there was nothing but the vehicle.

Not any vehicle, he abruptly realized. But a truck. A black pickup truck.

"Tucker? Are you thinking what I am?" Leanne's voice was full of concern.

"Oh yeah." As they drew closer to the black truck, he noticed the tinted windows. That made him pull off to the side of the road and kill the engine.

"It could be a trap," he said.

"Maybe," Leanne agreed. "But we can't just sit here. We need to check it out."

He reluctantly nodded and slid out from behind the wheel. Leanne joined him. "Stay back as much as possible. I'll take the driver's side, and you take the passenger's side."

"Understood."

He lifted his voice. "Police! Come out with your hands up where I can see them!"

No response. He moved closer, edging along the driver's side of the car. The tinted windows made it difficult to see, but he could just make out the image of a man slumped behind the wheel.

Leanne was approaching the passenger's side with caution, too.

Still fearing a trap, he stayed back while he reached for the door handle. To his surprise, the car wasn't locked. He quickly wrenched the door open, then put both hands on the gun, prepared to shoot.

Leanne read his mind and did the same thing on her side.

The slumped man didn't move. Edging closer, he saw the round bullet hole in the victim's temple. There was another guy in the passenger's seat. Tucker and Leanne locked gazes for a moment, before he moved closer.

He sucked in a quick breath when he recognized both men.

Kurt Watkins, the man who'd met with the deputies for lunch, and the driver of the silver truck.

And they were both dead.

FIFTEEN

Leanne held the new .38 in both hands as she opened the passenger's side door. Seeing the dead man in the passenger's seat, she realized he was the driver of the silver truck. There was a second dead man in the driver's seat. Kurt Watkins, who'd met with Gomez and Barnes at the restaurant.

"Both gunmen are dead?" She tucked her weapon into the waistband of her jeans.

"Yep." Tucker cast a wary gaze around the site of the black truck, as if expecting more shooters to converge on them. "Looks like the Gomez brothers are getting rid of witnesses."

She walked backward until she could see the license plate. The one covered in mud. "They're the ones who shot up the motel room. Black truck with tinted windows and a mud-covered plate." She sighed and shook her head. "I'm sure they were eliminated partially because they'd failed to kill me."

"Yeah." Tucker narrowed his gaze. "Watkins has a criminal record, and the other guy likely does, too. Easy enough to arrange for them to take the heat, throwing suspicion off the deputies. And now that they're dead, they can't point the finger at anyone else. Like the guy who hired them."

"We have to call this in." She winced at the thought,

knowing she'd be taken into custody. "At least we're in Travis County. I should be safe in that jail."

Tucker looked undecided, as if weighing his options. He took out his replacement phone and took a few pictures of the dead men and the black pickup truck, including the muddy license plate. Then he turned and gestured to their car. "Let's get out of here. I'll call this in as an anonymous tip."

She fell into step beside him, humbled by his willingness to continue putting his career on the line to protect her. "Okay, but you must know they'll eventually track your cell phone to the big box store where we bought it."

He shrugged and quickly slid behind the wheel. "Can't be helped. Besides, hopefully we'll have some time before they're able to find us."

She shot him a look of doubt as she clicked her seat belt into place, but let it go. If nothing else, they could ditch his phone and get another.

Yet his comment nagged at her. How much longer could they avoid the inevitable? Now that Watkins and the driver of the silver truck were dead, she wasn't sure how they'd find the connection they needed to prove the Gomez brothers were dirty.

Especially if they continued eliminating witnesses.

Like her.

A wave of despair hit hard. She tried to stay focused on scanning their surroundings as Tucker drove back toward Austin. Whoever had pulled the trigger should be long gone, but they couldn't afford to make any more mistakes.

Had kissing Tucker been a mistake? She felt herself flush. This wasn't the time to think about that. For all she knew, she'd be in jail by nightfall.

When they were far enough from the scene, Tucker made

the call to the authorities. He spoke in a low voice and only gave the barest of details.

"I just drove past a couple of dead guys in a black truck outside Cedar Valley." With that, he disconnected the call. Then he tossed her the phone. "Turn it off for a few minutes."

She did so, then stared down at it. "We still need to connect with Jackson."

"I know. Soon." He sighed and rubbed his jaw. "I'm not sure where to go from here. Our trap didn't work, and worse, we lost our best leads, Watkins and the driver of the silver truck."

Oddly, his dour mood concerned her. She was the one wanted for murder, and needed him to remain positive. "We're going to figure this out." She managed a reassuring smile. "They're panicking, or they wouldn't have killed both gunmen. They know we're onto them." She pursed her lips. "Maybe we need to track down Dominic Clark and convince him to turn on the Gomez brothers."

"I'd considered that," he admitted. "Not sure he'll squeal on his buddies."

"It's worth a try." She searched for another idea. Coming up with a strategy to find the evidence they needed helped buoy her emotions. They had God on their side, and much like David armed only with his slingshot, she would fight with the weapons that were available. "And don't forget the idea of heading to the canyons behind your grandfather's ranch. That's where this started. I can't help but think that seeing it again will spark some memories."

Although going through her apartment hadn't helped as much as she'd hoped, surely seeing the scene of the crime would be significant enough to help her remember.

Tucker nodded. "We'll discuss that idea with Jackson."

He gestured to the phone. "We've been on the road for a few minutes now. Try turning it back on. Don't answer any call that isn't from Jackson. You can see his number in the recent-calls list."

"Okay." She powered up the phone, setting it in the cup holder between them. Almost instantly the phone rang, startling her. When she saw Jackson's number on the screen, she hesitantly answered. "Hello?"

"Leanne? Where are you and Tuck?" Jackson was breathing hard, as if he was running. "I need you to pick me up, as soon as possible."

She eyed a passing sign. "We're still five miles outside the city, but we're on the way. Where should we meet you?"

More heavy breathing. "I'm heading for a strip mall on Barton Road. There's a restaurant on the far end. Can't remember the name of it, though."

She glanced at Tucker. "We're on our way," she repeated. "Are you safe?"

"For now." With that, Jackson ended the call.

"Are you familiar with a strip mall on Barton Road? One that has a restaurant on one end? I'm worried because it sounded as if Jackson was running for his life."

"I know where it is." Tuck hit the gas, sending their SUV surging forward. She bit her lip, understanding his need to get to his fellow Ranger. But they couldn't afford to be stopped by the police for speeding, either. "Jackson is smart. He'll be fine."

Being smart wasn't the same as being safe. The only thing she could do was to silently pray for God to watch over the three of them, and Marsh, Pops and Stacy, too.

Moments later, they were back within the Austin city limits. A sense of apprehension cloaked her. She felt as if they were going into the heart of danger, rather than escaping it.

Shaking it off, she picked up the phone and did a search on restaurants in Austin. There were far too many, but she sorted them by price, so the cheaper ones were listed on top.

"Buckley's Barbecue?" She glanced toward Tucker. "Looks like it's at the end of a strip mall."

"That's the one. I remember passing it now on our way to the Willow Brook Motel." A hint of a smile tugged at the corner of his mouth. "Figures Jackson found the closest barbecue joint."

She was glad he'd slowed his speed as they drove through the outskirts of the city. Glancing at her watch, she realized it had been nearly two hours since Watkins and his accomplice had slammed the motel room with bullets.

Her stomach rumbled with hunger. Even the image of the two dead men didn't seem to matter. Maybe it was the stress that fueled her appetite. Or the anticipation of a barbecue sandwich.

They drove through the city streets in silence. She imagined the local cops were still at the scene of the motel shooting, and would be for a while yet as they carefully picked through and examined evidence.

Like their cameras.

The phone rang again. Recognizing Jackson's number, she quickly picked it up. "Are you at Buckley's?"

"Yes, I have a booth in the back." He didn't sound as breathless this time, and she imagined he was glad to be sitting down. She wanted to ask what happened, but decided to wait. Tucker would want to hear the story, too.

Up ahead, she caught a glimpse of the large Buckley's sign. "We're almost there."

"Good." There was no mistaking the relief in his tone. "Thanks."

"See you soon." She glanced at Tucker. "He's in a booth in the back."

"Got it." He nodded toward the side street where an Austin PD squad car was waiting for the light to change. "I have a bad feeling they're looking for Jackson."

"If that's true, we can't stay at Buckley's." She dropped her tone, even though the cop in the squad car obviously couldn't hear their conversation. "I'll let him know to head out the back."

Ten minutes later, Jackson darted out of the restaurant and ducked into the back seat of the rental, a paper bag in hand.

Tucker didn't hesitate to drive away, glancing at the rearview mirror to see Jackson. "Do I smell barbecue sauce?"

"I brought lunch, and three water bottles." Jackson looked satisfied with his brilliance. "I wasn't about to leave empty-handed."

"Of course not," Tucker drawled. And she was glad that he didn't look as depressed as before. "Let's eat."

She accepted her sandwich and a water bottle from Jackson. "Dear Lord Jesus, thank You for this food and for keeping us safe, especially Jackson. Amen."

"Amen," the guys echoed.

The barbecued-rib sandwiches were messy, but Jackson had plenty of napkins. And as Tucker drove through Austin toward the interstate, she knew he was taking her suggestion of visiting the canyons behind his grandfather's ranch.

And she prayed that they would find the answers they so desperately needed.

When they'd finished eating and had left Austin behind, Tucker eyed Jackson in the rearview mirror. "What happened?"

"Things went well at first, especially after I showed them

my badge." Jackson sighed and ran his fingers through his blond hair. "But as soon the major crimes detective showed up, the atmosphere at the scene changed. By the way he looked at me with suspicion, I could tell he wasn't buying my story. When one of the crime scene techs yelled out about finding a broken camera, I decided to get out of there."

Tucker hiked a brow. "I can't believe they didn't pick you up within a few minutes."

"I waited until the major crimes detective went inside, and muttered something about needing to use the bathroom." He grinned. "I went into the lobby, out the back and then took off running."

If the situation wasn't so grim, he'd have laughed at the image of Jackson running down the street to escape. He sighed and shook his head. "Great. There's likely a warrant out for your arrest now, too."

"It was only a matter of time. After all, I was allegedly borrowing your SUV, and they'll eventually find our prints on the cameras." Jackson didn't look concerned. "Looks like you have a destination in mind. Care to share?"

Tucker quickly filled Jackson in on finding the two dead gunmen, Kurt Watkins and the unknown driver of the silver truck. He glanced at Leanne as he explained how they had heard the gunshots and headed out to search for the source.

The memory of their kiss returned in full force, but he ruthlessly thrust it aside. He couldn't afford to lose focus on the case.

Not when their hours outside of a jail cell could likely be counted on one hand.

"We're going back to the scene of the original crime." Leanne answered Jackson's question. "To the canyons behind the Rocking T Ranch."

Tuck noticed the surprise in Jackson's gaze and shrugged. "I'm open to other options, but I'm fresh out of ideas."

"Yeah, okay, but we can't just walk around in the middle of nowhere," Jackson said. "At the very least we need hiking and camping gear."

Tucker shook his head. The moment Leanne had mentioned going to the canyons to help her remember, he'd considered the best way to approach the area.

And that included sneaking back onto the ranch.

"There's gear at the Rocking T. I'm fairly certain I can find the old dirt service road." He glanced at the dashboard clock. "The problem is that we have a good three hours of driving ahead of us."

Three hours of being vulnerable on the road to every single cop from all counties who would be on the lookout for them.

"Good thing I bought lunch," Jackson muttered, leaning his head back against the seat. "Let me sleep for an hour or so, then I'll take over the driving."

"Okay." Getting a little sleep was probably a good idea, since Tucker suspected they'd have a long night ahead.

Using the GPS that came with SUV, he chose their route. He'd stay on the interstate for a while, since they needed to make good time, then head out on lesser-traveled highways.

The real danger would be when they hit Diamond County. He had no doubt that every available deputy would be out on the roads searching for them.

Good thing this part of Texas was largely rural. The Rocking T and their neighboring ranch, the Wandering Willow, took up several hundred acres. Hopefully, finding the three of them would be like looking for a needle in a haystack.

The trip took three hours and ten minutes. At the halfway point, they stopped for gas, more water and to swap drivers. He napped for an hour, then gave Jackson directions on how to find the old dirt service road. Unfortunately, the main road that wound around the back of the property wasn't in much better shape. He could see the entrance to the dirt service road up ahead.

"Wait!" Leanne's excitement was palpable. "That area over there looks familiar."

Jackson obliged by slowing the vehicle, then pulled over as far as he could. They hadn't passed another car in miles, which had been both a relief and strangely concerning.

The Diamond County Sheriff's Department should have been out in force. He'd expected to find them manning roadblocks, but there hadn't been any sign of them. It was as if they had driven into a ghost town.

"What's familiar about it?" Tuck asked as Leanne continued to stare out her passenger's side window.

"That rock outcrop over there." She gestured, and it took a minute for him to find the area she meant. The rock outcrop had a unique diamond shape, which must have stuck in her mind. "We need to get out and walk closer."

"Hold on," Jackson protested. "How far are we from the ranch? Maybe we should sneak in there first to grab some gear, then come back out here to explore the area."

Tucker scanned their surroundings. "That's the dirt service road, roughly fifty yards ahead. It's two miles long and ends where the old homestead used to be located. That spot is nothing but an empty space now, but if you go through the trees, you'll eventually reach the current ranch house and barn." He scanned the horizon. "We'll only have sunlight for another couple of hours. I vote we stay for a bit to make the most of it."

Jackson sighed and killed the engine. "Okay, let's check it out."

Leanne shot out of the car and headed purposefully toward the out cropping of rock. Tuck quickened his pace to join her, leaving Jackson to cover their backs.

"Easy," Tucker cautioned. "Be on the lookout for snakes and other critters."

She didn't seem to care about the threat of wildlife. Her gaze was fixated on the diamond-shaped rock. "I was here, Tuck," she said in a low voice. "I know I was here."

Maybe this would be the impetus for her memory to return. He strode alongside her, every sense on alert as they covered the rocky terrain.

The ground dipped, causing her to misstep. Thankfully, she didn't fall and offered a wry grin. "Sorry. Guess I should pay attention to where I'm going."

"Yep." To the left, he saw what appeared to be one of the canyons. He put a hand on her arm. "What about that area? Does that look familiar, too?"

She paused, taking in the scenery, and slowly nodded. "If I'm right about this location, the border checkpoint is another mile or two beyond that canyon."

He frowned. "The ranch isn't that close to the border."

"I'm not sure of the exact distance, but the checkpoint is at a road that leads to the border." She turned in a circle, then added, "The wilderness is deceiving. Maybe it's five miles. I'm not sure. I just know I was here." She waved a hand. "I remember waking up with a headache and seeing that diamond-shaped rock."

"Really?" His pulse quickened. "Maybe we should split up to search for the original scene of the crime."

"Wait." She reached out to grab his arm. "I ran for a while. I remember tripping over rocks and clumps of dirt."

She looked again at the rock then back to the canyon. "We may want to drive farther down this road toward the checkpoint."

He wasn't sure about that idea. "Won't there be a border patrol agent there? Maybe even a Diamond County deputy?"

Before she could say anything, a cloud of dust in the distance caught his eye. His gut clenched with trepidation.

"Tuck? Let's hit it!" Jackson's worried tone mirrored his concern.

Taking Leanne's arm, he turned to head back to the SUV. But a crack of gunfire had him ducking for cover.

A second crack of gunfire rang out and the metallic *ping* indicated the SUV was the target.

"Find shelter," he whispered, belly-crawling along the ground. The three of them were armed, but they were also out in the open without protection.

A small grove of scraggly looking trees were about fifty yards behind them. Farther from the SUV and the dirt service road that led to the ranch. If they could get there, they'd have a chance to survive this.

A brief chance. Having only three handguns against a stationary shooter with a scoped rifle wasn't good.

He and Jackson hung back, making themselves targets to protect Leanne. To her credit, she moved fast, slithering along the ground with fierce determination.

They made it to the grove of trees, but the dust cloud was bigger now, and he could clearly make out the outline of an approaching vehicle. A police vehicle.

They were trapped!

SIXTEEN

Leanne crouched within the trees, giving Tucker and Jackson room to join her. She was glad to be armed, yet she knew they were facing insurmountable odds.

"Marsh? We need backup!" Hearing Tucker's whispered words made her realize he was on his phone. "Stacy knows where the old service road is. Hurry!"

Having Marsh get there in time would help, but even then, she knew the shooter with the rifle had the upper hand. With a scope, he could see them from a distance and, if he was any good, pick them off like tin cans from a fence post.

"I'll surrender," she whispered. "If there's no other way out, I'll give myself up."

"Not an option," Tucker hissed. "They have no intention of letting you live."

Better to sacrifice her life than risk all three of them dying here beneath the shade of the rock. Rather than point that out, she grimly watched as the vehicle approached. The driver had slowed down significantly, likely concerned about being fired upon.

Their small guns didn't have nearly the range she'd have liked under these circumstances. But as she peered down the barrel of her weapon, she felt certain she could hit the vehicle's front end, disabling it.

How many deputies were inside? Not more than two, she decided. Two deputies and one rifleman.

Three against three didn't sound too bad. Except that the three of them were bunched up in one place. Yet even as that thought formed, she realized Jackson had moved away, going deeper into the trees, as if to approach the vehicle from another angle.

She moved silently through the trees, putting some distance between her and Tucker, while attempting to get a better view of the approaching vehicle. The dust made it difficult, but then the SUV bounced up over a rock, and she could see it was a Diamond County Sheriff's Department vehicle.

Resting her weapon against the tree trunk to steady her nerves, she fired three quick rounds at the front grill of the vehicle. Instantly, the SUV shuddered to a stop.

Two deputies bailed from the car, using the driver's side door, and crouched behind it for cover. One of the deputies shouted, "Leanne Wolfe, you're under arrest! Come out with your hands up!"

Interesting that he hadn't told her to drop her weapon. Maybe he didn't realize she had one.

"You're not as smart as you think you are," the second deputy jeered. "It's over. You're done."

The words echoed in her mind, and with a burst of clarity, she remembered the last time he'd said them to her.

You're not as smart as you think you are. It's over. You're done.

It had been Deputy Barnes who had said them. Barnes, who'd lunged forward to stab her, not expecting Troy to jump in front of her to protect her.

Because Troy had been in on the human trafficking ring, too. But at the last minute, he'd chosen to save her life.

A sense of calm washed over her.

"Maybe I'm not as smart as you," she shouted. "But you should know I mailed my cell phone to the feds so they now have the video I took of you and the two Gomez brothers letting the van of traffickers go through the checkpoint."

A long silence stretched between them. That she had the video was true, but sending the phone to the feds was an exaggeration. She'd buried the phone and her ID beneath a pile of rocks in the canyon during her desperate escape from Barnes and Gomez.

Then she'd fallen, rolling down the edge of that same canyon. She must have lost her weapon when she'd gone down. When she'd awoken, she hadn't been able to remember what had happened.

Other than she was in danger.

"Nice bluff," Barnes called out. "But if the feds had the phone, we'd be in custody by now."

"The phone was damaged. I had to get a new one to access the saved videos," she said. "I don't care if you don't believe me. The feds are onto you, and if you're smart, you'll take the opportunity to skip out of the country before it's too late."

A bullet struck the tree trunk inches from her face, making her duck.

Did Santiago have the long gun? Or the third deputy, Dominic Clark? She wasn't sure but was leaning toward Santiago. Back when she'd caught the deputies and Troy letting the van filled with women and young girls go past, she'd known that her father had stumbled upon this same operation.

And his going to his boss, Santiago Gomez, had cost him his life.

Two more rounds rang out, and this time it was the two deputies who ducked to avoid being hit. As much as she appreciated Tucker's and Jackson's support, they couldn't just stand here shooting at each other all day.

They'd likely run out of ammunition before the deputies did.

She turned to look behind her but couldn't see any sign of the Texas Rangers. That was when she realized Tuck and Jackson were doing their best to split up to take the deputies out of the picture.

For good.

A shiver of apprehension raced down her spine. She knew Barnes and Gomez were guilty, but it was asking a lot for Tuck and Jackson to take down other cops on her behalf.

"How can I trust you if I do choose to surrender?" Leanne asked, to keep them focused on her. "Why do I think I'll never see the inside of a jail?"

There was a brief pause, then Barnes said, "I promise we'll take you to jail."

Yeah, right. She reached up and jiggled the branch over her head, sliding away just as another rifle shot rang out.

"Tell Santiago Gomez to drop the rifle," she shouted.

Another shot rang out, and again she heard the *ping* of metal. Jackson or Tucker had gotten far enough around the vehicle to risk a shot.

"Get off my property!" The new voice was low and raspy, and it took her a minute to realize it belonged to Pops.

What in the world was he doing out there? Where was Marsh?

Another crack of gunfire followed by a strangled cry

indicated a bullet had found its mark. Scanning the area, she spied where Pops and Marsh must have been hiding.

"We have you surrounded," Marsh shouted. A second later, another gunshot rang out followed by another cry.

"They're down!" Tuck called with satisfaction. "Both deputies are down!"

That left Santiago Gomez and Dominic Clark, one of whom was likely manning the rifle.

Would he stay hidden, waiting for the moment to strike them all down? Or hightail it out of there?

There was only one way to find out. Taking a deep breath, she edged around the tree. Bracing herself for the pain of being shot, she ran out across the open field toward the police vehicle.

"Leanne!" Tucker's voice was a strangled cry just as she heard a crack of gunfire. She hit the ground and rolled to the car.

More shots were fired from the general area where Marsh and Pops were located, followed by a thudding sound, as if a body hit the ground.

Tucker sprinted toward her, his expression a mask of concern. But there was nothing but silence.

"Shooter is down," Marsh called with satisfaction. "I caught a flash of light from the sun bouncing off his scope."

"I'll check it out," Jackson called.

A long silence stretched as they waited for more gunfire. It never came.

As Tucker ran his hands over her arms and legs, making sure she wasn't hit, she looked up at the diamond-shaped rock.

And knew it was over.

Thank You, Lord Jesus!

***

How Leanne escaped being shot was a mystery, but Tucker was immensely relived she appeared okay. He wanted to shout, to ask what in the world she'd been thinking to draw the shooter out, but just then he saw a battered pickup truck pulling out from the dirt road.

Pops was leaning out the passenger's side window holding the shotgun, and he saw his sister, Stacy behind the wheel.

Marsh had the rifle, and even from here, Tuck could see the starkly apologetic expression on his face.

"I'm fine," Leanne said. "We need to check the deputies."

Tucker wanted to let them both rot, but of course that wasn't an option. Rising to a crouch, he rounded the vehicle to find Barnes and Gomez, both lying on the ground without moving.

Fearing a trick, he cautiously edged closer. A large pool of blood had formed around them, indicating they'd been hit. He'd fired at one, and he believed Marsh had taken out the other, shortly before taking the rifle shooter down.

And when he finally got close enough, he blew out a breath he didn't realize he had been holding.

They were both dead.

"We got 'em," Pops crowed. "We got 'em!"

Tucker sighed and turned to give Marsh an exasperated look. Pops was acting as if they still lived in the Wild West.

"I tried, but they insisted on coming along," Marsh said defensively. "Time was of the essence, so I didn't argue."

Pops could be stubborn. Stacy, too. Tuck decided there was no point in being upset as their arrival had turned the tide in their favor. "It's okay. Thanks for getting here so quickly."

"Tucker, you scared us to death!" Stacy ran out of the vehicle to hug him. "I'm glad you're okay."

"You, too." He hugged her, then clapped his grandfather on the back. "I can't believe you were riding shotgun."

Pops grinned. "I wanted to man the rifle, but Marsh insisted on being the one to use it. He was on the top of the truck roof, keeping an eye on things. The way he took out the shooter was amazing." Pops nodded with satisfaction. "Most fun I've had since I injured my hip."

Tuck shook his head ruefully, not sure how to answer that.

"Santiago Gomez is dead," Jackson shouted. "Marsh only wounded him, but it appears as if his fall from the tree broke his neck."

It wasn't the most satisfying ending. Tuck would have preferred all three men arrested, tried by a jury of their peers and tossed in jail for the rest of their lives.

But he hadn't started this gunfight. He, Marsh, Jackson and Leanne had only ended it.

"I'd better call Owens," Marsh said. "We'll need help getting these guys out of here. And we still need information on the third deputy, Dominic Clark."

Tuck nodded and glanced at Leanne. "Nice bluff on the cell phone video. You had me believing it."

"It wasn't a total bluff," she said, her blue eyes earnest. "When Barnes accused me of not being smart and that it was over, I remembered him saying that exact same thing to me. Right before he tried to stab me with the knife. Troy Gonzales was involved in the human trafficking, but he stepped in front of me anyway, sacrificing his life for mine." She turned to scan the area behind them. "I threw Troy's body at Barnes and took off. He fired at me but missed. I pulled out my gun to return fire as I kept running. I run five miles on a regular basis, and that helped me gain distance from them. When I was far enough away, I took some time to bury the cell phone and my ID along the top of one of the canyons. Right before I fell and knocked myself unconscious. I must have lost the gun rolling down into the canyon."

He grasped her arm. "You really have video of them committing a crime?"

"I do, yes." She managed a smile. "I wish I had kept the phone, but I was too afraid that I would be caught with it on me. I figured I might need it as a bargaining chip."

Impressed, he nodded. "Smart thinking." He scanned the horizon. "And even if we can't find the device you buried, the video should be stored in the phone's memory. If we get a new phone, you'll still be able to access it."

"Exactly." She ran her fingers through her tangled hair, and shot a dark look toward the fallen deputies. "We suspected these three, but I really hope Dominic Clark and others aren't involved in this scheme."

"Me, too. Once we get access to their cell phone records, we'll know who they've been talking to." He listened as Marsh made the call to their boss, requesting backup from any officer who was not part of the Diamond County Sheriff's Department.

It was over.

He was so overcome with emotion; he snagged Leanne's arm and drew her into a warm embrace. He buried his face in her hair for a long moment, thanking God for sparing her life.

Today, and back when this nightmare started.

"I'm glad you're okay," he whispered.

"And I'm glad you're not hurt, either," she whispered back, slipping her arms around his waist and hugging him tight. For a long moment, it felt as if they were alone, but then he heard his grandfather chuckle.

"Ah, Tuck? Boss is sending a chopper." Marsh bluntly reminded him they had an audience. "He's also sending several Texas Hill County deputies, too, to avoid bringing other Diamond County cops into the mix."

"Good." Tuck lifted his head, expecting Leanne to step back, but she didn't.

Marsh grinned. "I'll go help Jackson with Santiago."

"I'll drive Pops back to the ranch," Stacy added.

Pops looked as if he was enjoying the show, but reluctantly turned and hobbled back to the ranch SUV, favoring his injured hip.

"Let's get away from here," Tuck murmured, drawing her from the bullet-ridden police vehicle and the two dead men.

They walked toward the canyon, arm in arm.

Finally, he paused and glanced down at her. "Do you remember everything?"

"Yes." Her smile faded. "My father knew there was something going on, and reported it up the chain of command. Since Santiago was part of it, that information didn't go anywhere, and my dad was killed. I took up the investigation once I was assigned to replace him. I suspected Santiago and a deputy to be in on the trafficking, but discovering Troy Gonzales was involved was a shock." Her gaze was troubled.

"So, you were working undercover?"

"Off the books undercover and on my own, yeah. I hid near the checkpoint on my day off and must have gasped out loud when I saw Troy standing beside Barnes as they let the van through. I took off running, but they caught up with me." She sighed. "You know the rest. I pushed Troy's body at Barnes, knocking him off balance, and escaped. The fall into the canyon may have actually saved my life."

"When you woke up, you couldn't remember who you were," he said, when she'd fallen silent.

"Yes. I only knew I was in danger. I crawled out of the canyon and headed for this road." She gestured behind them. "When I heard gunfire, I knew I had to get away. That they were still after me." She rested her head against his shoulder. "God guided me to your grandfather's ranch."

"I know. And I'm thankful for that." He believed in the power of prayer, now more than ever. From the moment he'd seen the deputies closing in, he'd prayed for safety.

And God had answered their prayers.

"I owe you my life, Tucker." She pushed away to face him. "I know this is all part of your job, but I feel awful that you were put in the position of having to shoot the deputies."

"They didn't give us a choice. I knew they would kill you, Leanne. Especially once they learned about the cell phone video."

"Yeah, well, I still feel bad." She glanced up at the sky, where the sun was beginning its slow decent on the horizon. "Although I'm relieved the threat has been eliminated."

He wanted to pull her close and kiss her, but they still had one item of unfinished business. "Do you remember if you were seeing anyone on a personal level?"

She laughed, and he wasn't sure if that was good or bad. "I'm not involved with anyone, Tucker. I was dating a guy named Andrew who worked as a salesman. He told me to let it go when my dad was killed. To move on." She grimaced. "I knew then he couldn't love me the way he should. Meeting you made me realize that breaking up with Andrew was the best decision I ever made."

His heart soared with hope. "Oh yeah?"

"Yeah." She stepped closer, resting her hand on his chest. "The real question is why you're still single."

He sobered, realizing he was in the same position now as he had been with Cherry. "My job requires a lot of travel. It's not conducive to relationships."

She arched a brow. "Sounds like a cop-out. If two people are truly dedicated and committed to each other, they'd make it work."

He hated to admit she had a point. "My previous girlfriend cheated on me. And then blamed me because I was gone all the time."

"Her loss, Tucker. Besides, I have a feeling cheating is in her nature, especially if she's blaming you. I have no doubt she'll find another excuse to cheat on the next guy." Her smile faded and she added, "Count your blessings that you didn't marry her."

"I am counting my blessings, especially the one where God brought you into my life." This time, he did pull her into his arms. "I love you, Leanne," he whispered, then kissed her.

She clutched him close and kissed him back. And when they finally had to breathe, he lifted his head and pressed another kiss to her temple.

"I realize it's too fast," he murmured. "I hope you'll give me the time to show you how much you mean to me."

"It is too fast." She grinned. "But I love you, too. I feel as if I've learned more about you in the past two days than I did in six weeks of dating Andrew. You're a keeper. He was not."

"Ah, Leanne." He didn't have the words to tell her how much she meant to him, so he resorted to kissing her again. In his heart, he knew she would never cheat the way Cherry had.

He held her close until the *whump-whump* of a chopper could be heard approaching from the distance.

"The cavalry has arrived." Tuck wished his boss had taken just a little while longer so he wouldn't have to let her go.

"Good." She leaned back to smile up at him. "I'm anxious to close this chapter and move on with the next. With you."

"I love you." He stepped back, took her hand and turned to watch the approaching chopper. He wasn't sure what his future held, but he knew he was open to anything.

As long as Leanne was at his side.

EPILOGUE

Three weeks later...

When word had gotten out about how Leanne had brought down two Diamond County deputies and a supervisor within the border patrol, she'd been pummeled by calls for interviews. Turns out, Dominic Clark had been an unwitting participant in the scheme. Or so he'd claimed. He'd only admitted to loaning out his truck, nothing more.

Her phone video had provided the evidence they'd desperately needed to exonerate her, Tucker, Jackson and Marsh of any wrongdoing. And after she'd turned the video over to the authorities, it had popped up on several news stations, prompting the interview requests.

But even better, the van she'd recorded had been located, and several women who'd been brought across the border to be trafficked against their will had been found and rescued. There were other victims to find, though, but her video had saved a few of them.

Leanne was at a crossroads in her career. She didn't want to go back to working the checkpoint or to her prior role as a liaison in Austin. Her Austin apartment lease was up, and she hadn't renewed it.

Tucker had been splitting his time working and caring for Pops. She'd pitched in to help with his grandfather, which also gave her and Tucker time alone to talk.

She'd found her old SUV hidden in some brush near the canyon and had it towed and repaired. She was making the long trip to the Rocking T when her phone rang with an unknown number.

"This is Leanne," she answered warily.

"Ms. Wolfe? This is Acting Sheriff Simon Crow."

She tensed, wondering why on earth the temporary Diamond County sheriff was calling her. "How can I help you, Sheriff?"

"I would like to offer you a job," he said bluntly. "Thanks to your efforts, Sheriff Kern has resigned. In the meantime, I fired two more deputies in addition to the two we've already lost. Oh, and Dominic Clark resigned, as well. I would be grateful if you would consider signing on as my chief deputy."

Chief deputy? Her thoughts whirled. The previous sheriff had instantly resigned when the news of his dirty cops had gotten out. And now, it appeared as if the acting sheriff was determined to rebuild the department. "That's an interesting offer, but I'll need some time to think about it."

"Take all the time you need," the sheriff said. "I am ashamed to know my fellow deputies were breaking the law in the worst way possible. I could use someone with your integrity and bravery to help reform the next group of hires. I'll match your current salary with a ten percent pay bump."

"It's not the money, sir," she said quickly. "I appreciate your willingness to clean house. And I'll be in touch with my decision soon."

"Thank you. Take care." He ended the call.

Wow. She slowed to turn into the long, winding driveway of the Rocking T. She couldn't wait to share the news with Tucker.

He was hovering in the doorway when she arrived, and quickly swooped her into his arms for a tight hug and a kiss. "I've missed you," he murmured.

"I've missed you, too." She kissed him again, then noticed Pops grinning at them from the living room window. "Your grandfather is watching," she whispered.

"He's worse than a toddler," Tucker groused. But he took her hand and led her inside.

"You're beautiful as always, Leanne." Pops slapped his grandson on the shoulder. "What's wrong with you? Don't you know a keeper when you see one?"

Tucker sighed loudly. "Don't steal my thunder, Pops." He looked a little exasperated with his grandfather's antics. "If you'all don't mind giving us a little privacy?"

"I hope I didn't raise no fool." Pops gave her a secret wink, then turned and leaned on his cane to head to his room.

"I got a job offer from the Diamond County Sheriff," she said, still thinking about the unexpected call. "The acting sheriff wants someone with integrity to work with him on rebuilding the department. He'd like me to be his chief deputy."

"And what do you think about that?" Tucker's expression stayed completely noncommittal.

She realized he was giving her the chance to make the decision without any pressure. Going back to work the border wasn't appealing, not after the way her father had been killed. It was time for a change. "I think I'd like to take it."

A wide grin bloomed on his face. "That's great, Leanne." He dropped to one knee and pulled a ring box from his pocket. "I love you, and want to share my life with you. Will you marry me? I know my job requires me to travel, but my heart will always be here at the ranch with you."

"Oh, Tucker." She smiled through glistening tears. "I would be honored to marry you."

"Well, it's about time," Pops called from the doorway.

She couldn't help but laugh as Tucker rolled his eyes, took a moment to slip the ring on her finger then stood to wrap her into his arms.

"I'm sorry Pops was eavesdropping," he whispered.

"I'm not. I love you both, and Stacy, too." Leanne didn't mind Pops being there as a witness to their love.

She couldn't wait to become a part of their family.

* * * * *

If you enjoyed this book, don't miss these other stories from Laura Scott:

Soldier's Christmas Secrets
Guarded by the Soldier
Wyoming Mountain Escape
Hiding His Holiday Witness
Rocky Mountain Standoff
Fugitive Hunt
Hiding in Plain Sight
Amish Holiday Vendetta
Deadly Amish Abduction
Tracked Through the Woods
Kidnapping Cold Case
Guarding His Secret Son
Texas Kidnapping Target

Available now from Love Inspired Suspense!
Find more great reads at www.LoveInspired.

Dear Reader,

Thanks so much for reading my Texas Justice series. I'm truly blessed to have wonderful readers like you. I hope you enjoyed Tucker and Leanne's story. I've been having so much fun writing about these handsome and rugged Texas Rangers! I hope you'll stick with me through Marsh's and Jackson's stories, too.

I adore hearing from my readers! I can be found through my website at https://www.laurascottbooks.com, via Facebook at https://www.facebook.com/LauraScottBooks, Instagram at https://www.instagram.com/laurascottbooks/, and Twitter https://twitter.com/laurascottbooks. Please take a moment to subscribe to my YouTube channel at youtube.com/@LauraScottBooks-wr1xl?sub_confirmation=1. Also, take a moment to sign up for my monthly newsletter to learn about my new book releases! All subscribers receive a free novella.

Until next time,
Laura Scott

Harlequin Reader Service

Enjoyed your book?

Try the perfect subscription for Romance readers and get more great books like this delivered right to your door.

See why over 10+ million readers have tried Harlequin Reader Service.

Start with a Free Welcome Collection with free books and a gift—valued over $20.

Choose any series in print or ebook.
See website for details and order today:

TryReaderService.com/subscriptions